ALANA OAKLEY

BLOODSUCKERS AND BLUNDERS

An imprint of Enslow Publishing

WEST **44** BOOKS™

Cataloging-in-Publication Data
Names: Inkwell, Poppy.
Title: Bloodsuckers and blunders / Poppy Inkwell.
Description: New York : West 44, 2020. | Series: Alana Oakley
Identifiers: ISBN 9781538384862 (pbk.) | ISBN 9781538384855 (library
bound) | ISBN 9781538384879 (ebook)
Subjects: LCSH: Detective and mystery stories. | Friendship--Juvenile
fiction. | Vampires--Juvenile fiction.
Classification: LCC PZ7.I559 Bl 2020 | DDC [F]--dc23

Published in 2020 by
Enslow Publishing LLC
101 West 23rd Street, Suite #240
New York, NY 10011

Cover design and Illustrations: Dave Atze

Typesetting: Think Productions

CPSIA compliance information: Batch #CS19W44: For further information contact
Enslow Publishing LLC, New York, New York at 1-800-542-2595.

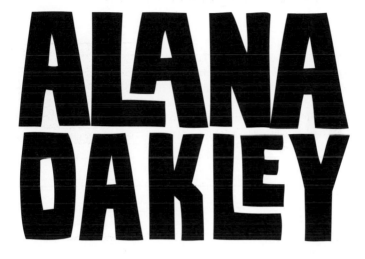

BLOODSUCKERS
AND BLUNDERS

An imprint of Enslow Publishing

WEST **44** BOOKS™

by Poppy Inkwell

For my three sisters:

Cristy, Lia, and Linda

CONTENTS

PROLOGUE

July 30

There were five people in Alana's living room. Only four were alive.

Yes. There was a **dead** body in the Oakley house. How could you tell which one? It was the only one not saying a word.

The living room was like a cavernous canyon with its very own echo.

CrudCrudCrud

Omigodomigodomigod

Wearesodeadsodeadsodead

To find out why there was a dead body in the house we need to journey back through time. Back to the day when Alana's new neighbors moved in.

The ones she thought were vampires.

SHUT. UP. AND. LET. ME. THINK.

... You heard her. Let's go... We'll come back and have a look at the body later.

CHAPTER 1

A spooky dump

February 6

There are always empty plots of land, condemned buildings, or abandoned construction sites that raise the hair on your neck and make you walk twice the speed as you go past. There was a house like this on the corner of the street where Alana lived. It sat across the road from hers with broken windows like baleful eyes covering a lesioned body. In contrast, Alana's home was an unremarkable double-story, semi-detached house in red brick. From the outside, you would never know it had a dozen botched-up D.I.Y.-jobs, or a Christmas tree permanently set up in her mom's office. It looked ... normal.

Alana lived there with her mom, Emma Oakley – freelance journalist, organizer of disastrous birthday extravaganzas and a self-confessed danger magnet. It was just the two of them now. Alana's dad, Hugo, passed away five years ago.

To the left of them was Mr. Peyton, with whom they shared a wall. Peyton was a grumpy retiree with a face like a walnut. He was obsessed with his leaf blower and kept to himself. "Harrumph," he would say by manner of greeting every morning before disappearing indoors. Alana never knew if it was from the effort of bending down to retrieve the daily paper because of rickety knees, gout, and a beer belly, or because he didn't like to talk. To their right was the polar opposite: new neighbor, Mrs. Whetu, hair in rollers and beady blue eyes peeled for gossip to dole out to "the gels" at the local R.S.L. And didn't Emma's friends, Katriona and Ling Ling, provide topics by the truckload! Forget their midnight raids of Sydney's Zoo to kidnap a penguin or their trip to liberate chickens … just visiting was enough!

"What did they wear this time, Ma?" the gels would ask, falling forward in expectation, mouths half full of Today's Special. Her audience's eyes would roll in lascivious glee as Mrs. Marama Whetu described every bizarre deed in intimate detail. They could never get enough. Although none of them had ever seen the women in person, they were confident they would know them in an instant...

...Emma Oakley – a petite Filipino woman with uncontrollable brown hair and dark eyes. She carried a large, patchwork bag with her everywhere and tended to walk around in a dream or scribble words on random surfaces (sometimes even the car!).

...Ling Ling Shu – a taller, slimly built Asian woman from Singapore who loved over-the-top accessories. Only her skin was a constant color (as pale as milk), while her eyes, nails, and hair changed more frequently than a chameleon.

...Katriona Karovsky – a blonde, statuesque woman from Russia, whose wardrobe from the 1970s showed off her classic pear-shaped figure when it wasn't in figure-hugging pelts and prints.

Yes, the gels would recognize them anywhere.

The houses on Alana's street stood in uniform attention like a row of soldiers, ready for duty. The derelict house stood out like a deserter. Alana Oakley, aged fourteen and five months, cycled past it every day to get to school. Today she slowed and sat on her bike, one foot on the curb and stared.

Someone was moving in.

The house had been empty for as long as she could remember. It wasn't hard to imagine why. It was huge and spooky in the way only old houses could be. The building had lost its fight against weeds and creepers that bullied their way through windows and cracks in the walls. The garden all but obscured the towering structure.

The house had its very own turret.

Not exactly a popular architectural feature in the Marrickville neighborhood. Or anywhere else in Australia for that matter.

The real estate listing in the agent's window had been up for so long it had faded to a whisper of blue:

This is a once-in-a-lifetime opportunity to own a substantial property in the coveted inner west city. This character-filled abode presents generous living spaces and elegant period details. Located only a stone's throw to vibrant Newtown, this is a haven of space and charm, possessing all the appeal of its original features. Whether you are looking for your first step on the property ladder, or an ideal investment, this is perfect for D.I.Y.-ers who enjoy the challenge of transforming a blank canvas into a dream home. Update or renovate this unpolished gem.

In other words, it was a dump. A creepy, old dump. Even in house-deprived Sydney where decent real estate sold at indecent prices, the house had refused to sell. And now it had. Alana was nonplussed. The new tenants must be desperate, insane, or blind.

Alana pushed off to restart her journey when something caught her eye. Alana was used to

Goths – wasn't Newtown full of them? – with their pallid skin, dark eye makeup, and gloomy daywear, but somehow the two youths in front of the old house looked almost *too* Gothic. Their sunken eyes were a little *too* bright and skin just a little *too* pale. They lounged against random bits of unpacked furniture scattered in the overgrown yard like a dazzling photoshoot for edgy urban-wear. The girl was perched on an ornate chair. She was younger than Alana, shorter (although not by much), and favored heavy eye makeup in a bruised blue to match her nail color. The boy looked older. He was leaning against an oak sideboard. *Early Victorian, if the shapes of the legs are any indication,* Alana thought to herself. She knew a lot about antiques. When you lived so close to King Street and its eclectic, vintage shops, it was hard not to. The boy had short, dark, spiky hair that hinted at a shade of burgundy. The style showed off his high cheekbones and light-colored, deep-set eyes. His severe expression stopped him from being handsome in the conventional sense, but he was striking in the way a cobra is and, Alana suspected irrationally, just as dangerous.

The new neighbors stared back, not moving. Alana was reminded of mannequins. An adult voice full of impatience, called from behind a teak wardrobe: "A little help here?" This galvanized the pair into action, but not before Alana felt she'd been weighed, measured, categorized, and discarded. What did the new neighbors see when they looked at her, Alana wondered. Was it her "average-ness" that put them off? She didn't have her friend, Sofia's, proud, aquiline nose or wild mane of dreadlocks. Nor did she have Maddie's mesmerizing eyes, the same shade of turquoise as the Coral Sea. And even though her friend, Khalilah, had dark brown hair like she did (minus Alana's magenta streak), Khalilah had a presence about her that demanded your attention, a charismatic air that drew you to her ... no matter what wacky scheme she was hatching. Up until that moment, Alana had been content with her nondescript nose, hazel eyes, skin the color of lightly warmed toast, and dimples which she'd inherited from her father, but now she felt ordinary. Ordinary and boring. Alana clutched her jacket a little closer, regretting the heavy book inside her school bag. Why did Sofia have to lend her a book on vampires? And why did the neighbors have to remind her of them?

Alana risked one last glance before she took off, just as the boy bared his fangs in a smile.

Fangs?!

Alana turned and pedaled faster than she normally would have because she didn't want to be late for the first day of school. Not because she heard a peal of laughter like fingernails against a chalkboard, followed by a derisory drawl: "You are *so* immature, Will."

No, definitely *not* because of that.

CHAPTER 2

Wishful thinking

Do you believe in vampires? Alana didn't. Not until that morning. The uncertainty snuck into her body like an ill-placed itch. It niggled and gnawed. She tried to ignore it – like she had the creepy home – but when least expected, the suspicion flashed in front of her like a cat pouncing on a darting shadow.

It was ... unsettling.

Shall we take another look at the body? Just a quick one? You can avert your eyes if you like while I describe it.

The body is thickset. It is heavier than it looks. (That had been a surprise.) It is dressed in conservative blue, arms by its side. A plain band of white marks the ring finger of the left hand. Hands that are the gnarled, knotted results of a battle with arthritis lost.

Magazines, a mug that reads "Instant human: Just add coffee," and a Pink Floyd CD have been shoved onto the floor to make room on the coffee table for the body. It doesn't fit. Or it does, but in the way a boy's shorts feel when he is ready for long pants.

The body is doing a very good impression of planking.

It is a stiff, after all.

"When I said I wished she were out of my life and could drop dead, I didn't think she would do this," somebody cries. The accusation is like a pigeon with a broken wing let loose among cats. It scrambles up the walls and down the curtains, now drawn to hide the spectacle from prying eyes. It limps across the wooden floors without gaining any real traction and spins like an ungainly ice dancer. And in its wake it loosens the lips of the spectators so the echoes resound again.

CrudCrudCrud

Omigodomigodomigod

Wearesodeadsodeadsodead

Be careful what you wish for.

CHAPTER 3

Bedridden blues

"I wish I were dead!"

While Alana was rushing away from her new neighbors, her mom, Emma, was in an apartment around the corner from her school to visit Ling Ling and Katriona. Although the melodramatic declaration ended on a very real-sounding sob, Ling Ling knew better than to be concerned. She took one look at the lump in the bed that was her roommate and business partner and threw back a pair of heavy, gold retroprint curtains. Ling Ling could easily survey King Street's traffic jam from here. The flat sat above their makeover salon, The Beauty Bar, which had unbeatable street frontage on Newtown's main road.

Down below, a semitrailer wheezed to a stop with an accordion's gasp and squeak. The driver waved his early morning coffee-to-go at Ling Ling in greeting. Ling Ling never outgrew the childhood habit of waving at strangers and now an odd collection of people waved every morning at the-woman-in-the-window whom they had never met.

"It's a beautiful day," Ling Ling said. The day was, in fact, grimy and dull. Even the marigolds in the window flower box looked depressed in sympathy.

The sudden show of light, however anemic, was too much for Katriona's pet cat, Jinx. He gave a yowl of protest from the foot of the bed, and took off down the stairs. He was surprisingly fast considering he only had three legs.

Katriona instinctively squinted under the covers against the glare of Ling Ling's outfit which was bound to be unbearably cheerful. Even with her eyes shut, Katriona was right. Ling Ling was two shades of lime green (hair), buttercup yellow (mini-overalls), and sparkly (hat). She was the very picture of Australian patriotism ... had it not been for the candy-striped thigh-highs in red and white. She looked like an Asian outback

Christmas elf.

The lump in the bed did not move.

"Looks like Arnie is doing his chin-ups," Ling Ling said temptingly.

Katriona's thin nose edged out from under the covers. "With shirt, or without?" came the muffled response.

They had given the bodybuilder next door the nickname, "Arnie," after their favorite "tough-guy" actor. And he had no idea he was part of the vista from Katriona's bedroom. His apartment was half a story lower than Katriona and Ling Ling's. He was so close they could change his TV channels with *their* remote, which was a lot of fun on a quiet Saturday night. The windows were angled so Katriona could only see random bits of his body jump in and out of frame. From what she could see he was very fit. The beginnings of a tattoo in red, blue, and yellow sat above the top of his gym shorts but it was too hard to make out what it was. Was it a flag? A Celtic symbol? Fake underwear? Katriona wasn't sure. Had she written the real estate listing for her own home it would have sounded something like this:

Café lifestyle — Located at the northern end of King Street, this unusually generous two-bedroom apartment offers New York-style city living plus an opportunity to work from home with a shop below. Cafés, restaurants, and bars at the door, easy walk to Sydney University and Royal Prince Alfred Hospital with unbeatable views of King Street and hunk next door. The ultimate Newtown address for ambitious, glamorous young urbanites.

In fact, Katriona had no idea if "Arnie" was Hunk or Hulk. From the look of his back hair Ling Ling guessed part-gorilla. But Katriona had seen enough of Arnie's muscled torso, arms, and thighs to believe it was nothing a good body wax in their salon couldn't fix. Who cared about his head?

Headless Arnie exercised every day to an audience of one, but for the first time since Katriona and Ling Ling had moved into the apartment eight years ago, Katriona did not scurry to the window to watch. Arnie, mindlessly counting the repetitions of his leg squats, had no idea today was Katriona's special day. Or that because of it, she was upset.

"I wish I were dead!" she repeated. "And I'm nevereverevereverever getting out of bed!"

The birthday girl was not in a party mood. That much was clear. Ever since Alana had told Katriona she could see "crow's feet" on her face, Katriona had gone a little crazy. She began chasing the "fountain of youth" and tried every beauty cream, face mask, and herbal remedy on the market. No treatment was too expensive or too far-fetched. But it seemed nothing could stop the March of Time and now The Day had arrived.

Ling Ling shrugged and retreated from Katriona's bedroom. On the way down she met Alana's mom, Emma, struggling up the stairs with a cake shaped like a large party hat. The cone was decorated with a capital "K" for Katriona, but in Emma's haste to prepare it, the "K" had been smudged into a capital "D." However, all that didn't matter because Katriona would never see her birthday cake. Not because she found the "Life begins at 30!"-banner offensive, or because it was too early for cake, but because Emma couldn't walk in high heels.

"Oh noooooooo!" cried Emma, tripping and flailing, as pink fondant and lilac cream smeared itself into a pastel arc along the wall.

Ling Ling dragged a long fingernail (painted with kumquat-colored koalas, of course), through the icing. "Hmmm, needs more sugar."

Emma landed on the bottom step, her poufy hair ensconced in the dunce-cap confection. Without it – and a lot more hair gel – she looked very much like Alana. They had the same kind of eyes, shaped like a cat's, but while Emma's were the color of dark chocolate, Alana's contained flecks of hazel that danced in the light. Although they looked similar they couldn't be more different. Alana, for instance, would never end up with smashed cake on top of her head. Emma sighed. She had made a real effort for the big occasion, much good it did her. Today's cheerful sundress was made for summer and sun, not sponge cake and icing. The outfit was a huge departure from the comfortable nightie and bunny slippers Emma wore every other day as she tapped on her computer churning out articles for magazines and newspapers. Getting Dressed Up was something she reserved for interviews (with rock stars and politicians and the like) and high heels for weddings. But it wasn't every day one of your best friends turned thirty.

"I'm-old-I'm-old-I'm-old-I'm-old-I'm-old-I'm-old!" Ling Ling and Emma heard Katriona moan from upstairs. "And I'm nevereverevereverever getting out of bed!"

CHAPTER 4

Sleeping Beauty

Cassy – Maddie's little sister – decided that she too was "nevereverevereverever getting out of bed" only she didn't know it yet. The four-year-old lay on a pile of blankets surrounded by hundreds of paper flowers made by her big sister's friends over the summer. Cassy liked to believe the flowers hitchhiked on a dandelion breeze and landed in her letterbox by magic. These, and other fanciful thoughts, filled her head as she lay, eyes closed.

"Again," she said.

Cassy's mom sighed as she looked at the pile of dishes in the sink and the mountain of dirty clothes. "Cass, I've read it three times already."

"Again," the little girl insisted, eyes squeezed shut.

And so because it was Troy's first day at school, and Cassy's first day without him, their mother sat down on the floor and read Cassy's favorite bit from *Sleeping Beauty* aloud.

"Ith that how it really happenth, Mommy?" Cassy said interrupting, wide-eyed and curious. Cassy's hair was fairer than her mom's or her big sister, Maddie's, with hints of gold in the curtain of brown waves, but she had the same eyes – all the Dawson children did – which were an aquamarine blue as changeable as the sea. Her chubby thumb fit nicely in the gap left by her two top missing teeth. She looked like a Christmas angel made of toffee.

Cassy's mom snorted and then smiled. "No, love," she said, thinking of her own life. "Not much chance of that happening." She got up to go. "Upsa-daisy then. Off you pop and play."

"I'm gonna wait a while," Cassy whispered. "Jutht in cathe."

Cassy was still there by tea time and wasn't interested in moving by lunch.

"Come on, you," Cassy's mom said later, a little brusquely, "you can't lie around all day."

Cassy's nose remained buried in her favorite book as she turned the pages. "I'm waiting for my printhe."

"Waiting for her prince?!" Auntie Mo scoffed, hours later. Hours where no amount of persuasion, bribery, or threats could shift Cassy's resolve. "Leave her. The sooner she realizes no one's rescuing her scrawny butt but herself, the better!" And with that, Cassy was left lying on her mound of blankets, clutching the book of *Sleeping Beauty*, surrounded by a paper pile of blooms.

CHAPTER 5

Vampires vs. Werewolves

Maddie had no idea her little sister, Cassy, was waiting for her prince in bed, just as Alana had no idea her mom's best friend had taken to hers in a fit of despair. Both girls were too excited to see Khalilah and Sofia on their first day back at school. After doing a quick physical – exclaiming over Sofia's latest good luck charm ... in her belly-button (!) and electric blue dreads, Khalilah's weight loss (2 kilos – yay, let's celebrate with a cream bun!), Maddie's new *old* violin, Alana's diminutive stature (now the shortest of the four) and magenta-streaked hair – they pored over the heavy book which Alana had borrowed over the summer holidays.

The book was a love story between a mortal girl, a vampire, and a werewolf and it brought back memories of the girls' own "love triangle" with Flynn Tucker last year. But because three of the girls had fallen for the Jet Tierbert-look-alike, Alana had called it a "love *square*." The love-struck girls had gotten over their crush and now saw Flynn as a brother ... at least three of the four girls did. Sofia still insisted Alana harbored secret feelings of her own for Flynn, but was too chicken to admit it.

"Who would you choose, vampires or werewolves?" asked Sofia, keen to find out which camp they belonged to.

"Vampires for me," said Khalilah. Her face had a cherubic mischievousness which her friends knew only too well. She wore her trademark hoodie and was sporting a new pair of glasses in rhubarb red. They were the reading kind. Her parents, Mr. and Mrs. Madzaini, were expecting Big Improvements in her grades as a result.

Maddie disagreed, lowering her violin. (People rarely saw her without it.) "No way! Werewolves for sure. How about you, Alana?"

Alana was too busy watching her new neighbors *glide* down the corridor of lockers toward the administration office. She gulped. *Of all the schools they had to choose to go to, it had to be hers: Gibson High!* For Alana it was a no-brainer. "Yep, werewolves. All the way," she said loudly. "And Will had better keep those fangs of his to himself!" she muttered.

But Sofia, who had also spotted the new students, and was eyeing Will, in particular, was quick to even up the vote. As the Gothic duo passed, Sofia pulled back her blue dreadlocks into a thick ponytail, exposing the lucky amulets she wore around her delicate neck. Alana swore she could see Will's nostrils quiver. She grabbed Sofia's arm and jerked her back. The violent movement made them stumble into another couple behind them. Coach Kusmuk and Miss Beatrice!

There was a growl.

Miss Beatrice, formerly a nun of the Benedictine Sisters from St. Bernadette's College, and now the girls' music teacher, was quick to place a pacifying hand on Coach Kusmuk's arm. "Raindrops on roses," she began to sing to the unhappy teacher.

It was a well-known fact that Miss Beatrice adored musicals and sang at every opportunity. Kusmuk's bulldog stance was the perfect trigger to launch into one of her favorites from *The Sound of Music*. "Where's your banana?" Miss Beatrice sang to the Roger's and Hammerstein melody. She traced her mouth in a semicircle with one hand as a hint. With reluctance, Kusmuk's lips turned up at the edges. The grimace looked painful. "There it is!" Miss Beatrice clapped. The pair of them moved forward, Kusmuk with a robot's smile and clenched fists, as Miss Beatrice's voice faded... "We simply remember our favorite things, and then we don't feeeeeel sooo bad..."

None of the four friends exhaled until both women were gone.

"What was all that about?"

Sofia was not the only one surprised. Had that really been Coach Kusmuk, their P.E. teacher? Alana had expected a sarcastic comment from her at the very least. The coach enjoyed inflicting Public Humiliation and Pain, especially upon

Alana who was Public Enemy Number One. It was a crown she'd usurped from Sofia, who'd called the coach a bird-brain the first day of high school in Year Seven. And mistaken her for another student. And a boy on top of that. No, Sofia's crimes had dwindled into insignificance since Alana knocked their teacher out in a "friendly" bout of kickboxing last year with Nurse Cathy in attendance. It didn't help that Flynn had untied the hand-knitted straitjacket (a gift from Mrs. Snell), while Coach lay unconscious. Luckily the cord of Nurse Cathy's defibrillator had been too short. There was no telling what damage the nurse would have done otherwise. The woman was keen. *Too* keen!

Alana hoped she stayed healthy enough this year to avoid visits to the clinic. And she hoped Coach Kusmuk was suffering from amnesia (if that explained her odd behavior), and while she was at it, she really hoped her mom would do something boring for her 15th later this year – after all, who organizes *kickboxing* lessons with Kusmuk for a birthday present?

While Alana was mentally adding a school transfer for their history teacher, Mrs. Snell, to her wish list, she noticed a sudden silence. Everybody was looking at her. Maddie was waiting for an answer, although to what question, Alana had no idea. She'd been too busy imagining Mrs. Snell's transfer to another *state*. Tasmania, maybe? The woman's thermal underwear would come in handy there. Alana sighed. It was nice to dream. But scholarship students like her didn't have that luxury. They had to maintain high grades if they wanted to get the education they couldn't afford. That was the simple reality for Alana, who came from a single-parent family. Alana's dad, Hugo, hadn't left them penniless, but Emma's earnings as a freelance journalist didn't leave much left over for extras.

"Sorry? What did you say?" Alana asked.

"Khalilah wanted to know if you were happy to hang out with Jefri sometimes, to help him settle in," Maddie repeated with a strange expression on her face.

"Of course!" Alana said. "I can't wait to meet him."

Jefri Madzaini, Khalilah's older brother, had been in Brunei to finish Islamic religious studies. Alana wondered what he was like. Would he be like Sofia's older brothers, all five of them as loud and as brash as each other? Or like Maddie's little brother, Troy, shy and sweet? Alana was an only child and, not for the first time, wished she had a brother or sister to call her own. Even though her friends complained that the ones they had were too bossy, messy, or annoying.

"Look, there he is!" Khalilah exclaimed, pointing at a boy exiting the same office into which Alana's new neighbors had disappeared.

Khalilah's brother gave a big, friendly wave that managed to knock a passing senior in the head. He threw a hasty apology over his shoulder before pounding over to them with frantic enthusiasm. He was a taller, thinner version of Khalilah, who gave the impression of being all arms and legs. His big, brown eyes were pushed deep into an eager face, like two raisins in an undercooked bun. The smile he gave them was like an enormous beam of sunshine.

"G'day!" he said, pumping everybody's arm up and down like a jackhammer. "I'm Doofus."

CHAPTER 6

Twinkle toes

Khalilah's mom and dad were not impressed when they discovered the practical joke their daughter had played on Jefri. But nothing Mr. or Mrs. Madzaini said could convince their son that the average Australian did not call people "blokes" or "sheilas," or that "Doofus" was not an English equivalent of the Malay *abang* (older brother).

"He's acting very strange," Mr. Madzaini whispered to his wife, while he prepared the evening meal of not-shrimps-on-the-barbie.

As if to emphasise the point, Jefri came flying through the kitchen with a cry. "That's not a knife, Dad," he said, slashing the air with a *parang* he'd brought from home. "*This* is a knife." The sudden appearance of the razor-sharp, 16-inch blade sent the newly-cut broccoli florets and carrots flying.

It was no surprise Jefri was the way he was. He had studied the material Khalilah had sent to Brunei with religious zeal. Books like *She'll be right, mate: How to speak Aw-strine in Thirty Minutes* and *From Never Never to Woopwoop: The A to Z of Aussie Culture*, as well as a stack of DVDs including *Priscilla: Queen of the Desert, The Dame Edna Experience,* and the classic, *Crocodile Dundee.* Thanks to his little sister, Jefri Madzaini called everybody "Possum" and was an expert in all things True Blue, Ridgy Didge, and Dinky-Di Aussie.

Oi! Oi! Oi!

"He'll figure it out," Khalilah said, blinking through her new glasses at her friends, unconcerned, "...eventually."

The three girls weren't so sure.

But they had little time to dwell on the matter as Year Nine was turning out to be Preparation For Year Ten and Life-Changing Decisions that Affect the Future.

"Really?" said Sofia. "I had no idea planning a career was so serious."

Maddie, who decided at age four that she would

perform with the Sydney Symphony Orchestra, looked at their substitute science teacher, Miss Metcalf (nose buried in another surfing magazine). She shrugged her shoulders. Wasn't it obvious?

The news put Khalilah and Alana into a slight panic. Unlike Maddie, their ambitions had thus far been limited to beating teams from the Soccer Academy and playing music together in their band, neither of which they saw as a life-long career path. But graduation, Sofia reminded them, and Year Twelve, was ages away yet, and by the way, what did they think of the new boy, Will?

Alana could not shake the memory of Will and his sister in the yard of their spooky house to say anything positive, and the arrival of someone even creepier made it impossible to do so. It was hard to imagine something scarier than a houseful of vampires moving into the neighborhood, or even Mrs. Snell teaching history, but there it was. In the flesh. In front of them. Standing where Coach Kusmuk should have been.

Was it the sequins? The frills? Or feathers which were the most frightening? Whatever it was, the new teacher had the same effect on everyone, except a boy called Colin, who moved closer to admire the woman's outfit. The woman's face had the powdered sheen of cracks filled in with putty. Her hair (under the feathers) was white and gelled firmly into the shape of a doorknob. She raised one hand-drawn eyebrow as she glanced around the group of gaping students before taking a delicate sniff of her perfumed handkerchief.

The Year Nines were squeezed into the Police Boys' Club classroom which doubled as a dance studio. Despite its location at the back of the main gym, however, there was a pervading stench of soggy feet. Although the gym was home to Coach Kusmuk's Boot Camp, the P.E. teacher was nowhere to be seen. Alana checked her schedule. No, she hadn't made a mistake. First and second period was *definitely* P.E.

"Good morning, Year Nine!" the peacock woman said brightly. "I'm Mrs. Cronenberg and I will be taking you this year for ballroom dancing." It was a voice made for dainty cups of tea and raised pinkies, but her announcement floored them like a sledgehammer.

Shocked whispers ran around the room. "Did she say dancing?" "Ballroom dancing?" *"What?"*

"As you may be aware," the teacher continued, ignoring the gasps, "next year is your Year Ten Formal. Traditionally, the school celebrates the occasion with dances accompanied by the school's orchestra –"

"So if we're in the classical orchestra, we don't have to do ballroom dancing?" Maddie interrupted hopefully.

"That is so. Although," she held up a warning hand as some music students began hissing in triumph, "you will ALL need to learn ballroom basics this year."

Alana's face fell. She played the electric guitar. There seemed little chance she could get out of this terrifying class. She hated to say it but she would give anything to see Coach Kusmuk walk into the room. There was a knock at the door. Alana looked up expectantly. Instead it was Will and Khalilah's brother, Jefri, who were new to Year Ten. They had been sent to learn the basic steps with the Year Nines. The contrast between the two boys couldn't have been more striking. One looked like a walking corpse. The other looked like an overdose of caffeine.

"Cheer up," Flynn whispered. "You might even like it."

Easy for Flynn to say. Flynn had been studying ballet for the last four years. He'd have no trouble with ballroom dancing. At first Alana thought ballet was an odd choice for a guy who could have chosen any sport or activity to excel at, but after spending more time with Flynn over the summer (a summer where Maddie had gone to her usual music camp, Khalilah was playing tour guide to family, and Sofia had moved houses), she'd learned that dance was Flynn's way of keeping his mother close, the same way Alana did by learning her dad's mother tongue,

French. It was hard enough Alana's father had died in a hit-and-run car accident, but she couldn't imagine being abandoned. Flynn's dad explained it by saying it was cruel to cage a butterfly. And so Ketut, the delicate Balinese dancer who had given Flynn his large, slanted eyes and fine bone structure, had danced out of the Tuckers' lives as softly as she had entered it. The only thing she took when she left was a photo of the four of them, arms around each other and laughing in front of Luna Park. That, and the light from her husband's eyes.

Mrs. Cronenberg's dance class forced Alana to move her body in ways that felt strange and foreign. Sofia shot her a sympathetic look as Alana tripped over her feet for the fifth time. Even Miller White, the year group's resident geek, seemed to be picking it up! (Admittedly, he *was* muttering about 45 degree angles and counter-clockwise turns.) Alana couldn't understand it. She was musical. She had rhythm. She could do the footwork in soccer. Why was it so hard?!

"Posture! Balance! Timing!" Mrs. Cronenberg called out. "All are very important ... Like so," she said, giving Flynn a little congratulatory clap. Alana made a face and tried again. "Take up the movements with your partners now, and listen to the music." To her horror, Alana was paired with Will. Mrs. Cronenberg gathered up her full skirt and swept over to the stereo system to cue the music. "Remember, the waltz is the epitome of elegance, poise, and beauty," she trilled.

"Perhaps that's why you're having trouble?" Will whispered in Alana's ear.

"No," she replied sweetly, taking great satisfaction in seeing her heavy boot crush his big toe. Not completely accidentally. "My feet are doing *exactly* what I want them to do."

"Remember, graceful sweeping movements, everyone," the dance instructor called out. "Lovely lines," she directed at Maddie and Colin, "although traditionally the *male* leads."

My two left feet. Dance class. Kill me now! Alana posted James a picture of her boots. Uncle James.

Where was he when she needed him? Probably taking amazing photos in some exotic locale, she reminded herself. James was her mom's work partner and took the shots that gave visual impact to Emma's words. Alana suspected he'd like to become more than just a work partner but so far had not made any moves on her mom. Not that Alana's moves were anything to rave about at the moment.

If you took off the boots, your dance partner would have a better chance of survival! James posted back.

That's the idea, Alana replied.

The Year Nine students shuffled and twirled as best they could, alternately giggling in embarrassment and jostling each other whenever couples got too near. Mrs. Cronenberg reminded them of the basic steps whenever they needed help. "No, forward with the left foot, side-step and close, then backward with the right foot, step to the side and close again. Yes, yes, that's it," she said encouragingly to Jefri. "Boys, please maintain a proper frame! Posture, posture, posture!"

"Excuse me, what is your name?" Mrs. Cronenberg asked, interrupting Alana and Will mid-step with a sharp tap on Alana's shoulder.

"Alana," Alana mumbled.

"Alana, may I?" Mrs. Cronenberg asked, smoothly taking Will's hand which Alana eagerly dropped. Will's hand was as cold and as bony as a dead fish. The dance teacher gave a little nod and Will moved forward with ease, expertly moving in a circular fashion as if born in another century. Then the new boy executed a six-count underarm turn which the teacher hadn't yet taught them, making Alana even more suspicious. *First fangs, now he acts like he knows stuff from a bygone era?* She felt a familiar tingle in the back of her mind. Something didn't feel right.

The music changed and the tempo quickened. Without missing a beat, Will spun Mrs. Cronenberg around so that her skirt swirled up, revealing two glittery heels. Their arms and legs became a blur as they charged about the room in a flurry of frills and feathers. Was it the cha-cha? The tango? The quickstep? Or perhaps a combination of all three? Whatever the dance was, Mrs. Cronenberg was very impressed and showered Will with praise. At the end of class, several Year Nine girls rushed to compliment him on his smooth moves. Will exited on a wave of flattery and floral deodorant.

"Crikey!" cried Jefri. "That bloke was pretty bonza, eh? I reckon I've got Buckley's Chance of getting as grouse as him but I'm gonna give it a burl, anyways." Jefri's head swiveled back and forth swiftly. "So, Possums, where can I get me some tucker?"

Khalilah put an arm around her big brother. "You know Jefri, people *really, really* don't speak like that here."

"Yeah, pull the other one, sis," Jefri chuckled. "It's got bells on."

Alana was prevented from leaving class by Mrs. Cronenberg who assigned her extra homework to improve her poise and balance. Alana sighed. *From Elite Squad to Dancing for Dummies.* She waved at her friends, who mimed that they would wait for her at the school cafeteria. They had a whole summer to catch up on after all. She wondered what Sofia's new home in Surry Hills was like, what new tracks Maddie had to share from music camp, and how Khalilah's outback adventure had gone.

There wasn't much for Alana to update them on regarding her own life. She had spent most of her time working at Katriona and Ling Ling's Beauty Bar for extra cash. She could now mix up a decent batch of honey-blonde highlights, and do the prep work for a full-body wax, but to be honest she'd spent most of her time tidying up and eavesdropping on clients. Alana was amazed by what people were willing to share. At least she had squeezed in a couple of cool circus classes, at the Addison Road Community Center, which more than made up for cleaning duty. Alana was able to add knife-throwing (fake, of course) and stilt-walking to her tightrope, unicycling, juggling, and trapeze skills. Although after Coach Kusmuk's training, the acrobatic work was almost too easy. It had been a lot of fun and she couldn't wait to show her friends what she could do.

She was reluctant to tell her friends about Flynn though, and his determination that she should listen to more than just rock. Alana threw a glance at her school bag where a "mixed tape" lay hidden with the book of vampires. According to Flynn, his collection of songs on the pen drive was part of Alana's "musical education" – tracks by the Beastie Boys, David Bowie, and John Coltrane. The memory of it made Alana smile. He didn't know it yet, but she'd made a collection of rock history music of her own – songs by P.J. Harvey, Janis Joplin, and AC/DC. She just needed to find the right moment to give it to him. While Mrs. Cronenberg demonstrated another exercise in poise and balance, Alana closed her eyes and got lost in an imagined Hendrix track.

When Mrs. Cronenberg finished her dance demonstration she was annoyed to see Alana's head thrashing up and down, playing air guitar, but the *boom, boom, boom* of a hip-hop beat interrupted any scolding she was about to give. The frills in her bodice twitched in irritation.

"Oh hey, sorry Missus, I didn't know you wasn't done yet," the owner of the boombox said.

Alana grabbed the interruption like a lifeline and injected more warmth in her greeting than it deserved. "Trân, my man!" she exclaimed. "How've you been?"

The youth she greeted was slight with an angular face browned to the color of teak. His eyes were much narrower than Alana's – so thin they disappeared when he smiled. The hair on the sides of his head was cut short with two zigzag lightning bolts shaved on either side. His T-shirt was printed with a montage of "retro cassettes" and his baggy jeans hung low on his behind.

"Woh, hey, it's Hotchickalana," Trân beamed. "How you goin'? How's your mom? You know she was a real inspiration to me. I was real bummed she had to leave but," he jerked his head at what looked to be a new batch of Second-Chancers – a name reserved for participants of the rehabilitation program run by the Newtown Police Boy's Club – "I'm following in her footsteps and sharin' the love, you know what I'm sayin'?" Alana wondered what the other two ex-Second-Chancers, Boris and Enzo, were doing now, and who they were sharing their "love" with. All three had been under her mom's care last year as part of Emma's community service (don't ask, but it *did* involve a high-speed car chase). Emma's parting advice – via a stone pillar, a leafy bush, and a boy in a leather jacket – was that the Second-Chancers should find their gift in life and use it for the benefit of others.

"You're teaching dance, too?" Alana asked Trần.

"Yep," he said with satisfaction. "Any time you want me to show you some moves you just let Trần-the-Man know. Headspins, some old school breakdancing or moonwalking ... I can show you how to really get down!" He did a demonstration.

A head full of feathers blocked Alana's view, making Trần sneeze. "Thank you, Mr. Man," Mrs. Cronenberg said, pushing Alana none-too-gently out the door, "but I believe Alana needs to *get down* to Gibson High!"

CHAPTER 7

Food for thought

By the time Alana made it to the school cafeteria there was little to choose from. The food technology classes must have been doing their unit on Care for the Elderly because all that was left was Chinese rice porridge and a strange looking dish labeled "junket." Alana grabbed a bowl of porridge, added some spring onions, peanuts, chili, a dash of soy sauce, and some chunks of "century egg" before scuttling over to her friends, who were finishing their meal.

After a lot of squealing and squeezing and giggling, the four friends took turns to fill each other in on their lives. Alana was not surprised that Maddie was working harder than ever on the violin. She knew of Maddie's hopes to study at Sydney's Conservatorium High School and they only took the best. Music camp for Maddie had been the perfect combination of hard work and fun. Sofia was tired from the house move but excited she had a new bedroom to decorate. Renovations to her home which sat above her dad's new restaurant were almost finished and Sofia promised they would get an invitation soon. Khalilah also had had a good time although it sounded like she was lucky to make it out of the National Park alive. While Khalilah was showing Maddie her battle scars from an overeager emu, Alana took the opportunity to glance around the cafeteria. It didn't take long to find her new neighbors who, unlike other students, were not eating, and sat as still as statues.

"Hey, what do you guys think of the new guy, Will?" she couldn't help but ask.

"I think he's pretty gorgeous," Sofia answered swiftly.

"Eye candy for sure," Maddie agreed with a smirk, "in a washed-out kind of way."

Khalilah mimed a thumbs up through a mouth full of food.

"Yeah, I know, right? I've never seen anyone so

pale before," Alana replied, careful to avoid their comments about Will's good looks. It wasn't the first time Alana and her friends had differed in their definition of attractive. Hadn't Alana been the odd one out when everyone else was slobbering over the teen heartthrob, Jet Tierbert, a couple of years ago? And then, Flynn, the year after that? "They've moved into the creepy house up the road, you know," she confided.

"Really! Wow, I thought for sure that place would get torn down." Sofia glanced over at the two teenagers. "I like his sister's nail color," she said, twirling her dreadlocks.

Alana fingered the strap of her school bag all too aware of the book on vampires sitting inside. "You don't think he's, you know," Alana struggled to find the right word, "strange? He's really good at that ballroom dancing stuff and so far I haven't seen him eat. At all…" *perhaps because he'd rather be drinking blood?* Alana resisted voicing her suspicion and she certainly didn't mention fangs. She would sound ridiculous, even to her own ears.

Maddie laughed. "Did you see what they're serving today? I'm not surprised he lost his appetite." She gave a teasing grin. "Not everyone likes moldy eggs like you."

"They are a very important delicacy in Asia, you know," interrupted Khalilah, coming to Alana's defense.

"Do *you* like them, Khalilah?" Maddie asked, surprised.

Khalilah made a face. "No way!" she said. "They're disgusting."

The four friends laughed and quickly shifted topic when Alana took out Sofia's borrowed book.

"Ooh, ooh, can I have it, please?" Khalilah asked.

"But you've read it already!" Alana protested.

"Yeah, I know," she said with a sheepish grin, "but I want to start from the beginning again. Here," Khalilah said, handing over an even thicker book, which made Alana grunt. "The sequel. After reading this," she declared, hugging the tome to her chest. "I just can't call vampires monsters anymore."

Alana eyed Will's table fearfully as they stood for their next class. "Oh, I don't know, Khalilah. I think the real thing would make you change your mind."

CHAPTER 8

A monster in their midst

Next class was English and drama. Their teacher, Dr. Olivier, fiddled with his bow tie as students found their seats. A fine bead of sweat made the top of his bald head look shiny. He dabbed at it with a large, spotted, orange handkerchief as he walked around the classroom.

All the lights went out. The distinctive scent of patchouli and musk that was Dr. Olivier's cologne blossomed in the sudden dark. A ghostly *mwa-ha-ha* echoed in the gloom. Somebody screamed. It sounded like Miller. There was a click. Light from a torch illuminated Dr. Olivier's face from below. It cast eerie shadows on his face and the wall behind him.

"This term we will be looking at the genre of horror," Dr. Olivier said ghoulishly. "So what better place to start than to discuss our greatest fears?" He turned the flashlight on them, one by one. "What makes your hair stand on end? What gives you goosebumps?" He whirled around and looked Alana in the eye. "What makes you tremble. In. Your. Boots?"

He flicked the torch at Alana's footwear so they appeared in a circle of light, like the star of their very own show. Alana obligingly made them shuffle and "twirl" which made the class laugh, easing some of the tension.

Dr. Olivier plunged them into darkness again. The flare of a match and the sharp tang of chemicals tickled Alana's nose. A candle in a jar rose in the air and was passed to the first table. More and more candles were lit and handed out so that their shadows on the walls flickered and danced.

"If we are to understand how horror writers use shared human emotions and experiences to inspire fear in their readers, we first have to articulate that which we fear most." He paused dramatically, smiled, and then continued in an ordinary voice. "There's a worksheet going around. Please take one and use it to write down some of your fears. Tomorrow, we'll be sharing in pairs."

It was strange working by candlelight but Alana was no longer surprised by the madness of her teachers' methods. Gibson High wasn't a conventional school. The longer she studied here, the more Alana was coming to realize just how unconventional it was. She certainly hadn't heard of any other school with their own collection of medieval torture artifacts. Or having to practice obstacle courses blindfolded. She wasn't even sure if Nurse Cathy was a qualified nurse. Her bookshelf was filled with titles like *Suturing in Seconds* and *Plastic Surgery: Common Myths and Mistakes*. It was little wonder students rarely got ill.

Alana glanced down at her list of fears.

#1. Coach Kusmuk. Coach Kusmuk was like a Chihuahua with shark's teeth and a dragon's roar. Yells of "Faster!" and "Drop down and give me twenty!" still made Alana twitch in her sleep.

#2. Mrs. Snell. History came alive, quite literally,

whenever she was around. The school's medieval torture artifacts were from Mrs. Snell's personal collection. The elderly teacher's rosy, chubby cheeks and snow-white hair, the wisps of which escaped her bun, tricked people into thinking of rainbows and pixies. Her stumbling shuffle made people want to help her across the street. But Alana, like the rest of the school, wasn't fooled. Just wave one of Snell's knitting needles in front of Flynn, if you don't believe me.

#3. Nurse Cathy. Her unbridled enthusiasm for human experimentation was the stuff of nightmares. A copy of H.G. Wells' *The Island of Doctor Moreau* (disturbingly well-thumbed) had recently been added to the clinic's library.

#4... Alana was about to add her new dance class to the list but hesitated. Dr. Olivier probably wouldn't appreciate any of her answers.

Time passed quickly and it wasn't long before the end-of-class bell rang. "Before you go," Dr. Olivier said over the sudden hubbub of excited voices, "some homework." He raised a hand to ward off the collective groan. "I'd like you to research a popular, fictitious monster. It could be Mary Shelley's monster of *Frankenstein* or Thomas Harris's Hannibal Lecter, anyone at all. Whoever or whatever you choose, I'd like you to describe their characteristics. How indeed, would we know they were a vampire, for example? What would give them away?" He looked around the class. The shadows contorted eerily by candlelight. "Could they, in fact, be sitting right next to you?" He loomed over one of the students who gave a nervous giggle. Dr. Olivier's voice dropped to a breath of a whisper. "Could there be a monster in our midst?"

Alana shivered as she felt her stomach flip. She felt she knew the answer to that one. To everybody's relief, the teacher switched the lights back on and then wished them a "frightfully good day."

CHAPTER 9

An artistic meeting of minds

Maddie's little brother, Troy, had grown taller in the past year, as if he'd been stretched on one of Mrs. Snell's torture racks. It was Troy Dawson's first day of school too. His tummy jiggled and churned at saying goodbye to Cassy, who sucked her thumb and wailed at the gate. They'd never really been apart before. Troy's hand disappeared into Maddie's when he met his kindergarten teacher, Mrs. Kent, and he only relinquished it when Maddie pretended to shoot at people's bottoms with her violin case. This made him laugh and the funny feeling in his tummy got a tiny bit smaller. When Maddie left and the funny feeling threatened to return, he jumped on it like it was an alien in a computer game.

Mrs. Kent didn't seem to mind that he spent a lot of time jumping and squashing things she couldn't see, or that he rolled around on the carpet while she told stories. Cassy would like school, he thought, as he spun like a spider monkey, first one way and then another. Troy took a break from these activities for art during lunch time, but only because the teacher's assistant, a massive mountain of a youth, was painting a huge mural on the playground wall. Enzo, as the boy introduced himself, set Troy up with paint and paper too. He gave him more when it wasn't enough. The pair of them worked side-by-side in a comfy-jeans kind of silence, Enzo pausing when he had to hitch his up which was every ten minutes, and Troy whenever he felt the urge to jump, which was almost as often.

"Like it. What is it?" Enzo said, looking at Troy's bold strokes of paint on the paper.

Troy looked down and explained. "That's Mom, working, cooking and doing stuff," he said, pointing at a figure surrounded by flames. "That's Cassy, crying because she's only four and not big enough for school," he said next, indicating a smudge of green sitting in a puddle of tears. "This is Maddie and her violin because practice makes perfect (she says), plus it's good for shooting bottoms." Troy then showed Enzo a rectangle with wheels which was rocketing off the paper. The circles were blurred with speed. "This is Dad. He drives a truck. He lives at home but not very often. Not as much as Khalilah (now pointing at a smudge in blue), who Auntie Mo says is around our house so much she practically lives there, but I reckon *she* can't talk coz she's around our house more than anyone else. Except Uncle Joe who can't move anymore because of his bunged-up knee. And his deaf ears which he turns off whenever Auntie Mo is around." Then Troy's voice dropped as he shared Uncle Joe's "secret weapon" of "poisonous gas" which always sent Auntie Mo scurrying for cover.

Enzo nodded in sympathy. He had people living at home who dropped in and out like it was a ruddy hotel (his mom's words, not his), and others who were good-for-nothing parasites, appearing when there was food to be had, but disappearing at the first sign of work. It was only recently that Enzo had decided to change from being a good-for-nothing parasite himself. Not because of his mom's harsh words, but because someone had told him – via a stone pillar, a leafy bush, and a boy in a leather jacket – that he should find his gift in life and use it for the benefit of others. A gift! Him? Enzo? Just the thought of it lying unopened inside of him made him feel a bit frightened, in a tummy-churning kind of way. But now here he was. Painting on walls and listening to others, and the alien feelings felt more and more squashed.

There were other things in Troy's painting. Aunties, uncles, cousins, and a flying soccer ball, which his big sister, Maddie, liked to play with her friends, Khalilah, Alana and Sofia. Troy had painted himself on victorious knees after scoring a goal. And Khalilah was eating a cream bun with a pocket full of jelly babies. Khalilah, in fact, looked a bit like a circus performer because she was also playing the flute and riding a skateboard at Bondi Beach. You could tell it was Bondi

Beach because of the seagulls in the picture which looked more like albatrosses in size. (Have you noticed how things that scare you always seem bigger than they are? Troy had.) Behind Khalilah was another car. It was full of mean-looking boys. They were chasing her and Alana who were now on bikes. The painting was looking more like a movie, changing by the minute. Alana was also playing the guitar. You could tell it was Alana because she was wearing big, spiky boots like a pair of angry echidnas. And there was a speech bubble floating above her with, "Don't mess with us!" in squiggles, because Troy hadn't yet learned to read or write. As if the boys in the car would dare, because now they'd come to Troy's neighborhood, Redfern. You didn't mess with Troy's turf if you knew what was good for you.

In Troy's painting, Sofia was drumming in the sky but she just managed to stay on the paper, and not drift off the edge into outer space, because of her lucky charms which acted like anchors around her neck, ankles, and arms. There was even a new one in her belly button (!) – a stud that Sofia said had more to do with style than luck. Although Sofia's dad *did* say that it was lucky she was too old to be put across his knee for a good hiding. And not to put anymore holes in her body that God didn't put there first. And not to wear crop tops at the dinner table either, because it put him off his food.

"And that's my family," Troy said when he was finished, puffing with pride.

When the pair of them looked at Troy's finished painting it was very, very long. It was very, very wide. And it was very, very big. It was twelve paper pieces across and twelve paper pieces down. It was almost as big as the wall Enzo was painting. Mrs. Kent said it was impressive. Troy's tiny chest puffed with pride. He didn't know exactly what the word meant, but he had a feeling it was deadly.

CHAPTER 10

A dance with death

"Posture! Balance! Timing!" All remained as elusive to Alana as gold at the end of a rainbow. The situation was so dire Mrs. Cronenberg decided Alana needed remedial work with the-great-and-fabulous Will.

After school.

At home.

The thought of entering the great, big spooky house full of suspected vampires filled Alana with dread, but inviting him to her own house wasn't an option either. Alana had just finished reading the original vampire classic, *Dracula*, by Bram Stoker. The author clearly stated evil was something that happened by invitation only. There was no way she would risk her mother's life by welcoming Will to her home. But could she go to his? *Alone?* Armed with nothing but a pair of spunky boots and half a kilo of organic garlic? When Alana's friends found out about the extra practice, though, she didn't have to.

"Maybe he can help me with *my* dance moves?" Khalilah said.

"Or even dance cheek-to-cheek?" Sofia said, twirling.

Alana felt guilty for feeling relieved. "Really? You'd come with me?"

Maddie wrapped an arm around Alana's shoulders and said with a wink, "Sure! What are best friends for?"

"Too right we will, Possum!" piped up Jefri. "We'll have a ripper of a time!"

It was a balmy afternoon in March when the five of them picked their way through the overgrown grass of Will's lawn. Alana noted that in the month since they'd arrived, Will's family had made minimal changes. The windows and walls had been repaired, of course, but the creepers remained and the house looked just as spooky as ever. The new knocker on the front door was equally forbidding, a large ring clenched in the teeth of a brass dragon. Sofia's knock on the wood was muffled, as if it were too thick for sound to make an impression. Despite this, the door opened before Sofia had time to finish. It was Will.

Will was in a black turtleneck shirt, black skinny jeans, and he wore gold-rimmed glasses fashioned into goggles. A velvet vest in plum stood out in stark contrast. He was like the ghost of a shadow. As lean as a wolf in winter. "Come in," he said, returning an old-fashioned fob watch to his pocket.

Even though the ceiling of the entrance hall was vaulted, there was little light. A wide staircase lay in front of them leading to the second floor. The carpet was blood-red. A tall Edwardian grandfather clock kept time with a grim *tick tock*. The rest of the furniture – Jacobean mahogany, Gothic oak – dragged down the corners of Alana's mouth. The interior was straight out of a horror film.

They turned right and moved from the entrance hall into a sitting room. It was what

Alana's grandmother would have dubbed a Room for Best. The best chairs, the best coffee table, the best china, carefully preserved in their antique splendor for display, not use. It was dimly lit like a museum, as if anything brighter might make them disintegrate. The air felt stale. They could taste the mustiness of the room on their tongues. The curtains were drawn even though it was still light outside. Will looked around at the space and then beckoned from a second doorway. There was another room. Larger, and more suitable for their purposes.

Alana lingered. Her feet followed their own thoughts. She was careful not to touch the washed-out photographs in their gilt frames, the cross-stitch cushions in faded thread, or the 1930s Art Nouveau lamps in the corner. She skirted around the brass sextant, barometer, and antique typewriter. The room was like a trip through a time warp. Alana also noticed strange contraptions that looked old but were really odd combinations of antique objects fashioned to a new purpose.

Curious, she thought to herself.

Without warning, a moose head jutted out from an alcove. Alana stepped back with a cry. It was then that she noticed the figure. It was seated in a 19ᵗʰ century Victorian parlor chair. Alana had seen one just like it, reupholstered in funky orange, in one of the antique shops on King Street. This one, in somber red velvet, looked like it was in its original condition ... with the original occupant. Alana's history teacher, Mrs. Snell, was old, but the woman sitting in the armchair looked *ancient*. The woman's forehead dominated her face. Large and domed beneath wispy hair that was scraped back tight. Her eyes were glassy. Her nose, hooked. She was a buzzard in human form. The clothes – a black cardigan with pearl buttons over a floor-length gown – were the disguise.

Suddenly the old woman stopped staring at the TV which wasn't on and pinned Alana with a malevolent glare. "This family is cursed!" she spat.

"W-w-what?" Alana stuttered. But before the

woman could say anything more, Will strode in.

"Oh, there you are," he said, eyes narrowing. His nose wrinkled in distaste. Alana clutched the bulbs of garlic in her pockets. "I see you've met Great Aunt Esme."

Alana gave a quick nod. She didn't trust her voice to speak.

"Poor dear," Will said, "Hasn't said a word in over fifty years."

Alana's head snapped back to look at Great Aunt Esme again. The old woman remained as still as a wax work. Had she imagined the outburst? Great Aunt Esme's eyes locked onto hers.

No. She hadn't.

The sound of a violin from upstairs helped Alana drag her eyes away. Maddie burst into the room to break the spell completely. "I love this piece of music," she said.

"I'll get my sister, Alice, to play the waltzes for us then, if you like," Will offered. "That will make dance practice more authentic."

Maddie picked her jaw from the floor. "So. Not

a recording," she said in a small voice.

In the adjoining room, Alice (Grade 6 violin, High Distinction, and only twelve!), played a variety of waltzes. Maddie was the only one who watched Alice's fingers skip lightly over the strings as her bow swooped and soared in time with the music. The others, meanwhile, winced as they watched Alana stumble after Will's feet like a blind zombie.

Alana felt as if hundreds of eyes were watching her every move. Perhaps there were. A hundred, I mean. The mounted moose in the "best room" had been the start. A jackalope, a bunyip, and a griffin stared down from one wall and a chimera, a dragon, and a unicorn from another. From an oak sideboard, the glassy eyes of a threadbare stuffed ferret watched them twirl.

Dead bodies.

They were surrounded.

Was it a sign of things to come?

CHAPTER 11

Dead to the world

Shall we take another look at the dead body? The one in Alana's living room? It is still there, you know.

The dead woman has folds of skin that sit at the base of her neck like a choker. It shows that at one time in her life she was even heavier. The skin on her face is paper thin. You can see veins. Capillaries. Like a map of the Underground which Khalilah used when visiting her cousin in London. Khalilah always has a cousin in London and they're always studying and having an Overseas Experience. It's a family tradition that has gone on for decades. At Madzaini reunions they reminisce about London's fish and chips. They exchange stories about getting lost on The Tube. They speak with a "pommy accent" and laugh like hyenas. *Har har har.* Khalilah hopes to go too, one day.

But I digress.

The woman's hair. It is so white it is almost transparent. If we watch the body long enough it looks as if the hair and nails are growing. This looks creepy but it is not true. It is an optical illusion. Dead bodies dehydrate and shrink, making the nails appear to be growing.

Her eyes. They are closed. But they manage to look accusing. As if the dead woman knows she shouldn't be here, lying on a coffee table in a strange living room, feet dangling indecorously off the edge. But the dead woman's anger – which the four girls swear they can feel like the heat from a furnace – is quashed by a loud sound of gas escaping.

Within three days of death the enzymes that aid digestion begin to eat you. This process of putrefaction releases noxious gases that make the body bloat. It forces the eyes to bulge. These scientific facts are of no consequence to the four girls in Alana's living room. For them it is simple. The gases that have built up in the body need to escape and they have...

The dead woman has farted.

The four break into hysterics. Their laughter is a huge release. The sense of relief is like a balloon. Their lungs swap fear for air. Until –

Knock knock knock.

"Hello! Anyone home?"

CHAPTER 12

It's all her fault!

When the "owner" of the dead body came to claim her, Ling Ling blamed Katriona. After all, it was Katriona who had rejected everything Ling Ling and Emma had planned for her birthday. It was Katriona who had not wanted birthday cake in the morning (smeared or unsmeared against the wall). It was Katriona who had not wanted a game of paintball, and it was Katriona who had not wanted three different spa treatments.

"That's what *you* wanted for *your* 30th," Emma pointed out to Ling Ling.

It was true.

But giving Katriona what she wanted, what she *really, really* wanted was not an option.

Neither of her friends could Turn Back Time.

Katriona kept her promise of "nevereverever getting out of bed" by staying in bed. For the rest of summer, all of autumn, and the beginning of winter as well. The Beauty Bar lost clients. Business went downhill. To make matters worse, the stock market fell with Ling Ling scrabbling after it. All her magic with numbers? Lost! Lost, until there was almost nothing left.

What do you do when you are almost bankrupt? *(Economize! Tighten your belt! Save!)*

Exactly! But that's *you*.

What Ling Ling did (secretly) was gamble.

Ling Ling gambled on greyhounds. She bet on backgammon. Mahjong. Card games. Football results. Horse races. Always "chasing-the-money, chasing-the-money, chasing-the-money." But Ling Ling was really only chasing her tail. After three months, she was so deep in debt that the only thing she had left was part-ownership of The Beauty Bar. And after losing another bet on a hamster, Ling Ling lost that as well. So when Katriona relented to get out of bed for a pilgrimage to see Kylie Minogue, rumored to be in Tasmania, Ling Ling jumped at the chance.

And by the way, don't tell anyone where they're

going...

...And if you see a little, old lady with white hair in a bun... RUN!

Darling Lala, (Emma wrote)

Auntie Ling Ling and I are taking Auntie Katriona on a road trip to celebrate her 30th birthday. Late, I know, but it's the only thing which will get her out of bed and hopefully out of the doldrums. Unless we don't see Kylie Minogue, in which case ... BUT we'll cross that bridge when we come to it. We will be back in plenty of time for the Big Game, so not long. (Wrong.) *Grandma dropped off some food – see the freezer – which should tide you over until I get back.*

Guess what? I bumped into our lovely new neighbors, you know the ones who moved in across the road, and they have promised to keep an eye on you. (What???!) *So nice to have some friends move in (finally!) who are of a similar age.* (Nu-uh!)

Miss you already.

Forever. For always. No matter what.

Mamadoodlekins

xoxoxoxoxo

P.S. I've sorted out that problem you were telling me about and the new neighbors are ecstatic to help. I won't say anymore because I don't want to spoil the surprise but I can't WAIT for your birthday! (This does not sound good!)

CHAPTER 13

The shark circles

Thirty minutes before Ling Ling started throwing random things into matching designer luggage – Destination: Anywhere-But-Here – Fok Wee Mung, a.k.a. Crazy Mother of Fok's Bakery in Sydney's Chinatown (a ten-minute ride from Newtown on the 428 bus, City to Canterbury Service, official stop Dixon Street, Haymarket), was looking at her Little Black Book through delicate, tortoiseshell glasses.

Had Fok Wee Mung been fifty years younger and ten kilos lighter, the Little Black Book might have contained a list of boyfriends, their contact details and perhaps a rating out of ten. Had Fok Wee Mung been a lover of literature and words, like Emma, the Little Black Book may have been filled with poetry. Or had Fok Wee Mung had culinary leanings, the Little Black Book might have described an old family recipe for mushroom and chicken feet soup. But alas, Fok Wee Mung, a.k.a. Crazy Mother, was none of these things. She was from Macau, a tiny peninsula sixty kilometers west of Hong Kong. A place which understands gambling better than Las Vegas, and the Little Black Book was full of tidy numbers in red and black.

Fok's Bakery was the legitimate front for the loan shark business that Fok Wee Mung operated. There were only so many steamed buns and mooncakes a person could sell in a day, after all. The Little Black Book detailed the amount of money Fok Wee Mung loaned. They were Substantial Sums. Fok's Bakery only dealt in Big Money. The names and numbers in the columns were written so small that Fok Wee Mung's very small eyes needed +4.0 lenses to see them. The clap of beads from an ancient abacus made one name in particular stand out. Fok Wee Mung tutted and repeated the calculation two more times to make sure.

Fok Wee Mung's hair was whiter than white,

sparse and thinning. She wore her hair in a top knot so that it looked like a steamed bun balanced on top of her head. Fok Wee Mung's skin was made fair with a skin-whitening face powder from Japan. But the real secret, she said, was a diet of homemade soy bean milk and pumpkin seeds which she cracked open with her teeth. *Crack* went the seeds. *Clap* went the abacus. All day long. She was very proud of her teeth which were Original. Made in China. The best porcelain chompers money could buy. But it was her eyes which gave Fok Wee Mung her nickname, Crazy Mother. Eyes which stared in two different directions. That, and a filthy temper which had seen hundreds of tea cups smashed against the wall.

"Please, I'll have the money next week. My baby needs milk!" "Please, my father has cancer!" "Please, the bank is repossessing my house!" Nothing moved her.

Fok Wee Mung did not mind the unflattering pseudonym. Or the whispered fear at the mere mention of her name. In her business, fear was an asset you worked hard to attain.

"Shu Ling Ling," Fok Wee Mung announced to the shadow waiting by her elbow. "It is time to collect."

...

What makes Shu Ling Ling's hair stand on end? What gives *her* goosebumps? What makes *her* tremble in her boots?

It isn't the dark.

CHAPTER 14

It's all *her* fault!

When the "owner" of the dead body came to claim her, Katriona blamed Emma. After all it was all Emma's fault that the pilgrimage to see Ms. Minogue was doomed from the start. After a certain high-speed car chase last year (no, really, I said don't ask), Emma had gone to Dodgy Dave's Car Yard. True to form, Dodgy Dave gave Emma a great little deal on a Kombi van that had seen one too many sunsets. The Volkswagen Camper had a full-length mermaid swimming up one side and a dolphin splashing down the other. Two large daisies encircled the front headlights and an even larger peace sign took center stage. Rainbows. Sunbeams. Fairy dust. It was a living work of art, claimed Dodgy Dave, and a steal at that. Gone was Emma's beloved car – may it Rest In Pieces – and with it all confidence she could drive.

"I know," Emma said, "I'll navigate. New GPS. It'll be fab."

It was not fab.

"Fab" – according to Katriona – is when you punch in the right coordinates and it directs you south, toward Antarctica, but not as far. "Fab" is when you stay awake for the trip and provide witty conversation, and glow-in-the-dark beverages with colorful mini-umbrellas. "FAB" IS WHEN YOU GET TO MEET KYLIE MINOGUE AND NOT GET CHASED BY THE POLICE FOR STEALING A GIANT PINEAPPLE.

It was a giant mango, actually.

WHATEVER!

It was true. Emma *did* put in the wrong coordinates and pressed the wrong buttons which sent the trio hurtling north into God's Country – the veritable WoopWoop of Anywhere-But-Here. When the GPS instructed Ling Ling politely to turn left, she turned left. When the GPS instructed Ling Ling politely to turn right, she turned right. Shu Ling Ling drove as if the very devil were nipping at her Jimmy Choo heels. She did not let Katriona's wailing of "I'm-old-I'm-old-I'm-old-I'm-old-I'm-old-I'm-old!" or Emma's steam train snores distract her from her mantra of Drive-Just-Drive.

Night followed day followed night and so it went on until suddenly there was only sky. And millions of stars. And no road at all, no matter what the GPS was insisting.

Ling Ling threw the empty container of Doze-Killer over her shoulder. It hit Emma awake. Katriona stopped mid-whine to take a breath. Ling Ling pulled over.

"Wah," she said as she fell out of the driver's seat onto the red earth, "so many bling bling, loh!"

CHAPTER 15

No, it's all *her* fault!

When the "owner" of the dead body came to claim her, Emma blamed Ling Ling. After all, it was all Ling Ling's fault they were lost, packed everything but the phone charger, and drove off in the wrong car.

The three women's worst fears were confirmed the next morning when the scorching sun replaced the blanket of stars under which they'd camped. They were like three lobsters cooked on both sides.

"My face!" Katriona screamed at the sunburn which puckered her skin and chapped her lips raw.

"My hair!" Emma screamed at the red earth caking her now-frizzy locks.

"My nails!" Ling Ling screamed and then stopped when she realized none of them were chipped. "Phew! That was lucky." She turned. "Aiyeh! Why like that?" Ling Ling gasped at the sight of her two friends.

A large bird of prey circled the trio who spent the next ten minutes running around the van, yelling and screaming. It could smell panic. It could sense fear. The odd-looking animals were obviously helpless and fast losing energy. It was only a matter of time. The bird was hungry. The three looked bony but the bird decided that combined, they would do nicely. One of them in particular, had a meaty rump that would last for weeks –

"Shoo! Get lost!" Katriona threw a large stone at the bird. Its huge wings opened as it moved to another branch.

"Oh, don't hurt it," cried Emma, ever the animal lover.

"Ummm, I have bad news," interrupted Ling Ling. Her long, fake eyelashes were clumped with red clay. They blinked nervously.

Katriona squinted at the sun and paused mid-aim as the bird readjusted its grip. "What? We're not in Tasmania? We know."

"That's not what I meant," Ling Ling said. "I don't know if it is bad news, actually." She bit her lip and paused. "What color is the poisonous one again?"

"Poisonous *what?*" Katriona closed her eyes against the sun's glare and threw a bigger stone at the bird.

"Snake," said Ling Ling.

Emma would not be consoled by the fact that, in the end, the snake – not poisonous, but not vegetarian either – had made alternative arrangements for lunch.

"It was us or the bird," Katriona reasoned.

Emma looked over her shoulder at the strange lump inside the python's body which lay motionless a couple of meters away. Katriona's stone had apparently found its mark and the bird had fallen to the ground like a gift from heaven. Emma shuddered. She could almost see the bird, watching her from within the snake's stomach. Except...

"*Caw!*"

The three women turned. On the branch of another tree was the bird of prey. Black. Smug.

Alive.

"See! I missed!" said Katriona.

Emma refused to be comforted. "So what's that, then?" she said, pointing at the lump still staring at them.

Ling Ling peered into the van. "Ummm ... has anyone seen Jinx?"

...

Beyond the snake, through the bush scrub and up the hill, Emma and her friends *were* being watched.

Just not by Katriona's pet cat, Jinx.

CHAPTER 16

A dark secret revealed

"Alana's mom has a hobby like that," said Jefri.

The seven youths were discussing Will and Alice's dad's pastime of "rogue taxidermy" – the artificial creation of mythical beasts from the stuffed parts of more than one animal. That explained the strange animals mounted in the room where Will and Alana had danced. The ones that made Alana lean away in revulsion, and Khalilah, Maddie, and Sofia giggle in half-fear.

Alana was the first to admit that Emma's bad luck with animals was catastrophic. Cats ran away. Guinea pigs had heart attacks. Guts the goat bit the dust after consuming a football. Even Choo Choo, Alana's hamster, had died from cannonballing out of a Vespa's exhaust. But at least her mom didn't stuff them and put them on display!

While Khalilah was trying to kick Jefri quiet (not easy, since the Victorian dining table with walnut veneer was four meters long and seated eighteen), so he wouldn't say anything else upsetting, Alice jumped up with a suggestion. "Let's play with the Ouija board!"

Will led them up the wide staircase to a winding, narrow staircase, which led to the turret room where the Ouija board lay on a small, round table. Nobody except Will and Alice had played the game before but Sofia had heard of it. The aim of the game, she explained in a hushed tone, was to connect with the spirit world. A ripple of energy ran through the group – part dread, part excitement. *A board which allowed you to talk with the dead?*

Alice showed them how it worked. Everybody, she said, had to place the tip of one finger lightly on the planchette, a wooden pointer which was flat and shaped a bit like a pear. The pointer would move around the alphabet to spell a word or point to basic answers like "yes" and "no," depending on the question. It was very important, she continued, that they showed the spirits respect, and lastly, the planchette had to point to the word "goodbye" before they finished the session or else the spirit would stay with them, *forever*. While Alice was condemning them to a lifetime of haunting, Will lit the candles of the antique brass candelabra. He then switched off the lights. Alana noted the turret room had no window. *Rapunzel would have no hope escaping here*, she thought. *Then again, neither do we*, Alana realized. There was only one exit. Khalilah gave a squeal as she felt something tickle her ear. Maddie, as it turned out.

Jefri rubbed his hands in anticipation. "Come on, don't be a wuss," he chided. "Let's get on with it and play this doovalacky, thingummyjig, whatsit."

Seven fingers rested on the planchette. Alana felt a cold prickle of fear tap-dance down her back.

"Are there any spirits present?" Alice asked the room.

The planchette didn't move.

"Are there any spirits present?" Alice asked again.

The planchette stayed where it was.

Will shifted with impatience. "Are any spirits with us?" he said loudly.

The candles flickered. Shadows on the wall stretched and grew long. Then the planchette began to move.

Y.E.S.

Will's voice rose in excitement. "How many spirits are there?"

The planchette moved again. Its movement was undecided. At first it moved toward the number five. It veered suddenly to the right toward eight and then swooped in the opposite direction. It settled on a number with a jerk.

1.

Alana shot her friends a look. *Are you moving it?* her gaze said, but everybody shook their heads. If the planchette was moving it wasn't because of *them*.

"Thank you for gracing us with your presence, oh Spirit," Will intoned, eyes closed in concentration. "What would you like to tell us?" All eyes were glued on the planchette as it was dragged from one letter to the next, dragging their fingers along with it.

W...

O...

O...

F...

Sofia jumped up and ran from the room with a shriek. Maddie, Alana, Khalilah, and her brother, Jefri, were not far behind. Down and around the spiral staircase the five of them fled. Down the wide staircase, past the grandfather clock, and through the entrance hall. Free!

Almost...

"Friends?" said a hunched figure in black, blocking their getaway at the front door. The man would have been taller if he could have straightened his back. The wiry hair that escaped from his bowler hat was as dark as midnight and his gaze cut through them as sharp as a scalpel. He had the same hooked nose as Great Aunt Esme and the same unnatural pallor as his children. The man could only be Will and Alice's father. "Please, stay for dinner," he urged, revealing two rows of sharp, pointy teeth. "Tonight is steak tartare!"

"No, thank you. Goodbye," they whimpered, beating a hasty retreat to Alana's home.

Alana's nice, boring, and spirit-free home.

Safe at last.

Or were they?

CHAPTER 17

A spirit reaches out

Once Sofia calmed down long enough to stop sobbing, she was able to explain why she was so upset. Maddie's reassurances that it was just a joke and Khalilah's claim that Will or Alice must have moved the planchette, fell on deaf ears. The message, Sofia insisted, was real.

"I should know," she sniffed, "since I murdered him."

!!!!!

!!!!!

!!!!!

Sofia twisted her mood ring. It was something she did whenever she was anxious and now the ring was the color of crude oil, thick with murk and sludge. Then Sofia reminded them of an evening long gone, of fingers jumping through candle flames and talk of fire. Did they remember? Yes, all but Jefri said because he was not there, they did. How could they forget last year's mystery arsonist setting Sydney's schools on fire? Everyone wondering, would their school be next? For Alana, the memories were particularly poignant. Hadn't she spent most of the year stalking their friend, Flynn, thinking he was the culprit, to find he was only guilty of protecting his brother instead?

While Maddie's violin, Khalilah's pet cat, Sushi, her diary and pillow, and Alana's mom sat in an imaginary pile of Things Saved, Sofia was hiccuping and sobbing hard. It was some time before she could speak again. "And remember," Sofia whimpered, "I'd said that if there was a fire and I had to choose what to save, I wouldn't take Nostradamus because Mom or Dad would bring him, so I would save my lucky charms, my drumsticks, and my favorite T-shirt instead?" They nodded. Sofia buried her face in Jet's (now-soaking) face in printed 100% cotton and howled. "Well...THEY DIDN'T!"

Sofia was convinced that Nostradamus, the

mongrel stray the Luciano family saved from the animal shelter, had crossed the spiritual planes to say, "Woof!" There was nothing anyone could say to persuade her otherwise.

CHAPTER 18

Emma strikes again

Sofia's parents, Mr. Luca Luciano, newly awarded 1-star Michelin chef and Dr. Nicolette Luciano, a chemical engineer from the University of New South Wales, were more philosophical about Nostradamus's demise and their subsequent move.

"The poor dog was half-blind," she said.

" – lost his sense of smell, so dinners were tasteless – " he shuddered.

" – and don't forget, he's been on Death's Door ever since we rescued him – " they agreed.

The fire had certainly set a number of things in motion. Like looking for a place with enough room for five growing boys. And somewhere with more privacy for Sofia. Or creating a space where Luca Luciano could work from home (a rooftop herb garden, living space, restaurant, and research and development area in the basement kitchen). On top of which, after Emma's disastrous visit to Luca's restaurant, *Gastroniment*, last year (again, don't ask, but customers were seen *fleeing* the premises), reinventing oneself had become an Economic Necessity. Thus, it was with mixed feelings that Sofia invited her friends and Emma to visit the new family home in Surry Hills which was nearing completion.

Ignore the dark façade of the restaurant at street level, with its chrome trim and smoky glass oozing discretion and excessive zeroes.

Ignore the interior with its rich velvets, decadent brocades, and references to Marie Antoinette's boudoir.

Ignore the cavernous basement which resembles a scientific laboratory, truffle oil and sea jelly beans barely visible through a miasma of scented dry ice.

Ignore the rooftop garden from which you can observe street art being created on Surry Hill's warehouse walls.

Ignore Sofia's brothers and their bedrooms of rolled up socks and boxer shorts forgotten under beds.

What we're really here to see is Sofia's bedroom. Entering the room is like diving into a gypsy caravan. Your first impression is of rich reds, blues, and gold. Things tinkle as you brush past. The air is heavy with incense that is clearing the air of negativity as we speak. The girls leap onto Sofia's queen-size bed which is smothered in satin throws with velvet trim, crocheted blankets and hand-stitched cushions in brocade. It is like being swallowed by a bejeweled marshmallow. Lucky talismans litter every surface. Good luck statues cavort on a nearby shelf. The only thing missing is a crystal ball.

The room is a far cry from the cupboard under the stairs where Sofia used to sleep, a bedroom she inherited from her oldest brother. Sofia's new room is everything you'd expect from a person who wears lucky amulets, rubs Buddha bellies when worried, or consults the stars for glimpses of the future. Still, Alana half-expects to see a whiteboard somewhere, filled with indecipherable equations, because apart from being a devout believer in all things Alternative, Sofia is also incredibly gifted in math and the hard sciences. That's why she and Miller, a friend of Alana's from last year, take extra classes with Mr. Hornby. Mr. Hornby with his warm, brown eyes and permanently flushed cheeks is the first person to have swept away Sofia's fear of numbers. Since then, Sofia has never looked back.

"I don't need a whiteboard, silly, I use my head!"

It is the kind of comment that makes Miller weak at the knees.

As the four girls inspect Sofia's room, Emma is carrying out her own inspection. Luca Luciano is trying to remain calm as she does this. He repeats the mantra from last week's yoga session silently in his head. He wants to close his eyes to block distractions but worries he will be unable to see what Emma is doing next. As it is, he misses his wife, Nicolette's, frantic hand signals. The kind of gestures that say: *"Behind you! The knife! She has a knife!"*

Only it is not a knife.

It is something much worse.

It is a hand drill.

Imagine the next scene in slow motion. Emma reaching out to secure a screw which rises from the wall's surface, like a pimple begging to be squeezed. Luca's arm stretching up toward Emma's hand drill with an hysterical: "Noooooo!" Emma's toes gripping her high heels as she gauges the distance with one eye closed, and an overly-optimistic: "Almost there." Nicolette's hands as they rush to cover her mouth, and the squeal of: "Watch out, Luca!" as he dives down and away from the spinning power tool. The spinning power tool which Emma drops as she clutches air and tumbles down the stairs...

I didn't mention the stairs.

There are a lot of them.

One for every fracture in Luca's body *when he cushions Emma's fall.*

CHAPTER 19

Law and disorder

Alana's experience with hospitals had never been good. Not the quality of care, of course, which was always impeccable. But she knew she'd been too often when ward orderlies knew her name, emergency room staff greeted her with a: "What happened this time?", and medical staff gave her mom suspicious glances. That's what happens when you have a mom who likes to Think Big every birthday. Thanks to Luca, Emma only suffered light bruising. Luca Luciano, however, was wheeled away on a stretcher, his body bent at awkward angles like a wooden push puppet with extra joins. Mr. Luciano was yelling and screaming and possibly kicking, although it was hard to tell. When they next saw him he was much more subdued, largely because of the body cast that included a head brace immobilizing his jaw and a decent dose of morphine. His similarity to the resident patients in Nurse Cathy's clinic sent a shudder through Alana and her friends.

The doctor left strict instructions that Mr. Luciano receive only two visitors at a time. Emma took the opportunity to slip away to find the perfect gift to say sorry. It was all her fault! She should never have worn those heels. She felt terrible! The hospital was decorated with children's drawings of brightly colored eggs and spring flowers, reminding Emma that Easter was around the corner. As if to confirm it, a life-sized bunny bounced along the corridor leading a noisy rabble of young patients. At second glance, Emma realized the children were chasing the mascot with ferocious intent. Emma cocked her head. There was something familiar about that rabbit...

"*Boris?*"

The bunny rabbit screeched to a halt and jumped back to cower behind her. The group of angry children threatened to overwhelm them both. Emma shook her head. There could only be one reason why a group of under-9s were baying for blood.

"Okay. Hand them over," she said.

Former Second-Chancer and now Boris-the-Easter-Bunny threw the contents of his brightly-colored basket into the air. A shower of chocolate eggs rained down to the children's delight. Boris snatched up a decorated egg in pink foil. Emma took it from his oversized paw to give to a child, only to be rewarded with a sharp kick in the shins. The pint-sized lynch mob let out a cry and shook their chocolate treasures in the air before retreating, victorious, to their ward.

"A *bunny*, Boris?" she began, hopping and rubbing her sore leg. She was unable to continue her when-I-said-you-should-find-your-gift-in-life-and-use-it-for-the-benefit-of-others-I-didn't-mean-this lecture, because who should round the corner but the same woman who had lectured Emma on the same day, one year ago. Only *her* lecture had sounded more like, "Stay away, Ms. Oakley, and KEEP away."

Judge Debnham!

Even though Boris was in full-body costume, and it was unlikely the judge would be able to tell she was in violation of keeping away from the former Second-Chancers, Emma wasn't risking it. Emma spun around and away from the *click, click, click* of Debnham's sensible heels into the first door she came to (Room 38A) and slammed it behind her. Boris, not quite giving up on free chocolate, bounded off in the opposite direction.

Emma's heart raced as she watched Judge Debnham *click, click, click* past her from the safety of the glass window embedded in the door. She glanced at her watch. Ten minutes. In ten minutes it should be safe to run to the gift shop and back upstairs to Luca. But a closer look at her watch made her realize that in ten minutes the gift shop would be closed. Drat!

For the first time since entering it, Emma looked around the room she had escaped into. It was a standard hospital room in a private ward.

TV mounted in the corner, large windows, white walls, peach-colored synthetic blinds, hospital bed, white bedsheet covering patient, and a container of enormous, yellow, get-well flowers on the bedside table...

Exactly ten minutes later, Emma Oakley, using the vase of sunflowers courtesy of Room 38A (conveniently deceased) as cover, scurried to Room 47B where Luca Luciano was lying – arms and legs suspended in midair like a broken marionette doll. Visiting hours were over. The Luciano family had gone.

Luca's eyes, the only part of his body he could move, stretched wide at the sight of her.

"Luca, I'm so sorry, terribly sorry. These stupid heels," Emma said, grimacing at the offending shoes. "I brought you a present, though –" and with a flourish, revealed the cheerful blooms. Luca's reaction was an eye-popping series of grunts that she mistook for excitement. "Aww, I know. They're beautiful, aren't they?"

Grunt, grunt, grunt.

"I'll put them close by so they can be the last thing you see at night, and the first thing you see in the morning," Emma said, shoving the flowers into his face so he could get a really good whiff, before placing them on his bedside table.

Squeal!

Exactly three minutes later – after Alana collected her mother from the room like an errant runaway, griping about visiting hours and Mr. Luciano needing rest – the sneezing began. Violent sneezes that racked Luca Luciano's body and made his body spasm in agonizing fits and starts.

Emma's gift *would* have been perfect if only Luca Luciano hadn't a severe allergy to one *Helianthus annuus*.

Common name: Sunflower.

CHAPTER 20

A truth stranger than fiction

The upshot of Luca Luciano's injury was that the opening of his new restaurant had to be delayed. But delays cost money. The move cost money. Renovations cost money. Daily living costs money. And the hospital cost money too. Thus against Dr. Nicolette Luciano's better judgement, and without her husband's knowledge, the new restaurant opened in secret, and its reputation, like all good secrets, spread like wildfire.

Brothers was the new restaurant's unofficial name. It swiftly became the hip hangout after a hard night clubbing. Celebrities snuck in through side doors and enjoyed intimate dinners and late night snacks. The Young and Beautiful disappeared behind the smoky glass famished and reappeared replete. The secret behind all this success was as baffling as it was unlikely... Sofia's *brothers* were the new chefs.

Sofia's five older brothers, Carlo and Monte, (university studies deferred), Dmitri, and the twins, Pepe and Bob, had never had much time or respect for their father's revolutionary methods of cooking. That he was known throughout the world for making culinary inroads in unchartered territory did not impress them. Theirs was an almost Neanderthal attitude to food. Me hungry. Me eat. You cook. Only now it was, You hungry. Me cook. You eat. With the important addition of, *You pay.*

The menu at *Brothers* was dictated by the basic tenet that empty stomachs need filling. And what better way to fill them than with comfort food? In their father's lavish new restaurant, equipped with all the accoutrements and extra cutlery associated with Fine Dining, the five audacious cooks served up dishes like macaroni and cheese, fudge brownies, and deep fried chicken, only they renamed them, Garbo Load, Chocolate Rehab, and Death Wish. The sumptuous surroundings heightened the meals' appeal as the diners' stomachs took nostalgic trips down Memory Lane and remembered the pleasures of home cooking.

Money began to trickle in. And then it poured.

The sounds of success were muted from the upstairs living space where Luca Luciano was slowly and painfully recuperating, but not even the soundproofed walls and being two floors up could conceal the vibrations of a jackhammer. Curious, Luca navigated his way down the stairs with all the grace of a tank. The body cast allowed minimal movement of his shoulder and leg joints, and from his torso wafted the unmistakeable stench of unwashed flesh. Luca despaired of his nose ever recovering. He clutched at the bedroom wall, spun counterclockwise down the hallway, and then thudded step by step until he reached the lower level, panting. When he arrived he could not believe what he was looking at.

People were lounging and laughing and drinking from recycled jam jars and eating... *What were they eating?* It looked like the kind of meals his wife sneaked to the kids when they were little.

The quick fry-ups and stodge his sons begged for after he'd served up exquisite delicacies created in his lab. His eyes took in the clientele and saw that there were more than a few familiar faces in the crowd. Familiar, and some of them famous.

"...I'm *luhving* the juxtaposition of über-luxury and *cuhmfort* food which elevates the concept of the-body-as-temple and, by virtue, transforms the home..." A voice was declaring over the babble in the restaurant. Luca knew that voice. He knew it belonged to an obnoxious bow tie, flamboyant fedora hat, and sparkly suspenders. He knew it was celebrity foodie Pakiri Sabantham, as sure as he knew the size and shape of the birthmark on his wife's back. A food review by Pakiri Sabantham could make you or break you, in this fickle industry, and it was for this reason Luca and his team had been known to agonize for weeks before deciding what to serve. And yet what was Sabantham eating now? What was that on his plate? Was it? Could it be? Was Sabantham really eating *a French fry sandwich?* Luca smacked his hand on his forehead and keeled over with the weight of the cast, but not before hearing his wife call for an order of "Roadkill" and a "Brickie's Special."

Luca Luciano found out it is possible for a day to go from bad to worse.

Ex-Second-Chancer Boris had ditched the rabbit suit and Moved On. He applied to *Brothers* and got the job. The job was as the Gofer. Boris was required to go for this and go for that: errands, deliveries, anything required. To Luciano's surprise, Boris, the long-haired, leather-jacketed lout (first impression) turned out to be a handy person to have around. He could source almost anything and got the best prices for the best produce. His only little quirk was a rubber chicken, which went with him everywhere. It was a useful item for demonstrating asphyxiation, if Sofia's family had but guessed.

The Luciano's were glad to employ Boris, the Imbécile (going by the embroidery on his leather jacket), for the lucky rubber chicken alone because it always guaranteed something extra "on the house." But he had other redeeming qualities, like the ability to think on his feet, not ask questions, and accept cash-in-hand below the minimum wage. So when Boris saw Luca Luciano in his body cast, unconscious, he did to him what he did to all deliveries: transferred him to the basement.

"More weird stuff," was his philosophical take on the matter.

Thus it was to the sound of a jackhammer (the answer to the mysterious vibrations) that Mr. Luciano gained consciousness, propped up against five shelves of toilet paper. Luca's sons were putting the finishing touches on a "Brickie's Special." The dish moved upstairs via a dumbwaiter and then the chefs – his sons! – started on the order of "Roadkill" by jumping on a motorbike (designed to move on the spot), and running over a plate of food. In the laboratory side of the kitchen, Luca's startled gaze fell on a boy whom he had never seen before. The boy had weird eyes that threatened to fall off the sides of his face and odd glasses. Luca was not to know that the boy was one of Sofia's classmates. He was not to know the boy had an IQ of 286. Nor could he have any idea the boy's heroes included the scientist Humphry Davy (inventor of the miners' safety lamp), who was well known for testing chemicals on himself to the point of choking (!) while calmly monitoring his heart rate.

All Luca saw was Four-Eyes running around the room fanning his mouth. Then his eldest son, Carlo, dipped a spoon into the same pot and swallowed a spoonful. Within seconds he began to do the same. Monte and Dmitri followed suit. The twins, Pepe and Bob, joined in the fun.

Sofia watched her five brothers and Miller run around – yelling, swearing, and sweating – with arms folded against her chest. Then she rewrote the evening's specials:

> *Are you up to the challenge?*
> *Put some hair on your chest!*
> *Finish one plate of the Brothers' Tongue-*
> *Melting Curry and win a dinner for two.*
> *Terms and conditions apply.*

When Luca Luciano woke up the next morning, back in his comfortable bedroom, he heaved a sigh and chuckled silently to himself: *What a strange dream...*

CHAPTER 21

The heart wants what the heart wants

While Sofia spent the first three months back at school juggling multiple roles – maître d', marketing manager, bookkeeper – Maddie focused on one thing. A chair. This was not the storytelling chair of her little brother Troy's kindergarten teacher. Nor Mrs. Snell's electric chair of electrocution fame. (Execution assignment due: Monday.) Maddie had her sights set on the First Chair in the Middle School Orchestra. A role reserved for the best violin player. Concertmaster. Right-hand wo/man to the conductor. Soloist.

(Soloist!!!)

There was only one problem.

Alice.

Maddie became obsessed with violin practice now that there was Alice, two years her junior, playing almost the same grade, and with special permission to join the Middle School Orchestra. Twelve-year-old Alice with her deathly pale skin, Goth gear, and freakish fingers that made arpeggios look effortless. Even Troy's excited descriptions of school couldn't distract her. Or the fact that Cassy, her younger sister, had pretended not to move from her makeshift bed in weeks.

Maddie practiced violin first thing in the morning and last thing at night. She practiced in between bites of lunch, all weekend, and in her sleep. She did everything humanly possible to be the best violin player she could be. But would it be enough? Enough for The Chair? The chair of her dreams? Maddie wasn't sure. The Year Ten violinists were moving on to the Senior Orchestra next year and making room. Room for New Blood like Maddie who had been waiting for what seemed like forever. Maddie, who had never wanted anything more in her life.

But there was only one problem.

Alice.

...

"Any idea," Alice asked Alana during music one day, in a voice that put Alana's teeth on edge, "if that guy, Flynn, is taken? I heard you and he are a bit of an item."

Alana watched Alice's tongue emerge with the lightning flash of a lizard's. An image of Alice's teeth sinking into Flynn's neck came unbidden to mind. It made Alana's protective instincts thrust into overdrive. (NOOOOOOO! KEEP AWAY! MINE!) So she began a tirade about Flynn and his "lame" taste in music, his loser of a brother, and less-than-masculine pursuit of ballet. All said with a knowing smirk and snicker. Alana was proud of her thespian performance, until...

"If you're finished with my *lame* music then you won't mind giving my pen drive back," said a voice.

Alana felt her guts spill on the floor in spectacular slow motion as she turned.

Flynn stood with his arms crossed. He was his usual careless self: shirt untucked, tie askew, hair an untidy mess Alana wanted to reach out and sweep back from his face. He towered over Alana, especially since, unlike him, she hadn't grown much over the holidays. His eyes were stormy for a moment before turning cold and hard. Like a kaleidoscope of gray that goes blank. The realization of what she'd done hit her like a slab of concrete. The memory of their summer laughter turned taunting. All hope of giving Flynn her own collection of music... gone.

"Mmmm, yummy yummy," breathed Alice from behind, in a voice only Alana could hear. "One person's trash is another person's treasure."

And screaming that Flynn wasn't trash, and would never *be* trash, in Alana's head, made no difference at all.

CHAPTER 22

And the truth shall set you free

While Sofia became fixated with food and Maddie with furniture, Khalilah developed her own obsession at the Bondi skate bowl. Khalilah loved rap music and the iconic beach appealed to Khalilah for its sun, surf, and hip-hop culture. The combination of graffiti art and skaters held irresistible allure. Last year, at the skate bowl, Khalilah had met a friend of Alana's, a Cambodian boy called Trần who showed her how to use a skateboard. Trần-the-Man with his beatbox groove, impromptu raps, and a total of six fingers.

"What happened to your hand?" Khalilah boldly asked him one day. Trần took one look at Khalilah, the girl he'd taught how to "take-off" and "glide" on his beat-up skateboard, and realized with a jolt that he didn't want to feed her one of his usual stories. The ones where Trần was a raging kung fu master, fighting off five gangsters with machetes, or a fearless surfer evading a shark. For once, he wanted to tell the truth.

"You know they call it the Vietnam War, but it didn't only happen in Vietnam," he began. Trần looked up to find Khalilah watching him with her warm, brown eyes. Watchful. Listening. Genuinely interested. He went on. "There was fighting in Cambodia and Laos, too. Not that I was alive when it all happened. This was like, in the seventies or something." The way he said "seventies," it was as if he was describing one of Mrs. Snell's history lessons. As old as medieval times.

"After the fighting stopped, and even after all the soldiers left, people kept getting killed." Khalilah's eyes widened. "Or they ended up like me." Trần held up his hand. The right one, where only a thumb and forefinger remained. "I was only a little kid when it happened," Trần's lips twisted as the memories surfaced. "Mom and Dad warned me not to play in certain parts of the land. Said it was dangerous. They farmed only where it was safe. But I never liked to listen. Still don't, to tell the truth," Trần glanced up briefly and continued when he saw the encouragement in Khalilah's eyes.

"So, I found this bit of metal which was half-buried in the mud and I tried to dig it out. Lucky for me it was only a tiny piece of a partially exploded landmine." When Khalilah looked confused, he explained. "Like a bit of a bomb, not a whole one." He laughed hollowly. "I wouldn't be alive if it had been whole. Some days I wish it had."

Khalilah leaned forward, alarmed. "Don't say that!"

"It's true," Trần said, giving her another of his twisted smiles. "My sister came running when she heard the explosion. She was always soft on me. Hated to see me cry and I was screaming my head off —" Trần took a deep breath. "She ran over another landmine trying to get to me." He stopped, unable to go on. "Didn't make it," he said in a choked voice.

Trần looked out at the ocean but Khalilah knew he was seeing something completely different – Cambodia – his home country where, even today, possibly six million landmines lay buried across 46% of the country's villages, and 40,000 people walked around without a limb.

"You want to know what the funniest thing is? My first name is Heng. It means 'lucky.' Lucky me," Trần said, not sounding at all lucky. "I got put up for adoption. I got a second chance in a new country with my auntie's family. Only they didn't know they were adopting a loser." At this, Trần raised his damaged hand to his forehead in a vicious salute. He looked sideways. Khalilah was still there. She hadn't run or moved away in revulsion. A part of him was surprised. Trần's voice dropped to a bitter whisper. "You know sometimes when I pick a fight I *want* them to beat me up. Beat me up so bad until there's nothing left. I deserve it."

Khalilah had no answer for this. No words

of comfort came to mind. No witty remark to disguise the pain. But she did have a cream bun. It was squashed and a bit out of shape from being in her pocket, but it was a cream bun all the same. Khalilah offered it to Trần and he tore off a bit from the end with a grateful smile. His right hand was like a pincer, holding it firm, while the cream fountained up through the pastry.

Khalilah stretched out her arm to make an "L" with her left hand. It looked just like Trần's, and she held it in front of her face. She gazed at it thoughtfully and traced the shape with her right forefinger. "L could be for 'lick,'" she said, licking off a white blob of cream that was on her thumb. "L could be for 'lucky,'" she said, tracing the shape again, "because you met me." Trần smiled. "L could be for anything, but it definitely isn't for 'loser.'" Khalilah forced Trần to hold up his hand too. It was larger and darker than hers with three scarred stubs. "You know what I think?" Khalilah asked. "I think L is for 'life,' because that's what *you've* got, and your sister wouldn't have wanted you to waste it. Come on," she said, urging Trần to his feet. "You're going to teach me how to ride this skateboard again. We may as well give the tourists something to laugh at."

Former Second-Chancer Trần never talked about how he lost his fingers with Khalilah ever again. But he was sure that meeting Emma, Alana, and therefore Khalilah, had given him his *real* second chance. A chance to look at his right hand – an "L" which he'd thought could only stand for "loser" – in a new way.

CHAPTER 23

Double mystery

Khalilah and Alana spent most weekends at Bondi Beach watching skaters ride the wind as a reward for soccer training. The Bondi skate bowl was the perfect place for this. While old men in faded fisherman's caps and three day's stubble played board games by the sea, and seagulls snapped up wayward scraps, the two friends watched the youths and their boards tumble through the air.

At any time of the day or night, the Bondi skate bowl was a frenzy of activity. Skaters liked to practice their aerial stunts at the bowl and make them more and more daring. At the end of autumn, a mysterious new skater arrived and took skating to another level, with stunts and tricks that others began to emulate. Their arrival thrilled Khalilah.

The skater was a mystery because they never showed their face. True, the crisp winds blowing off the sea held a new chill that made you shiver, and fewer people flopped on the sand to work on their tan, but even so, three beanies and two scarves was overkill. It was from this bizarre headdress that two dark, deep-set eyes peered out, scanning the cement for an opening before storming down the slope in a clatter of wheels, faster and faster until the momentum sent them flying and twisting in midair. At least, this is how Trân described it to Khalilah.

"I can't believe I missed it!" Khalilah groaned, as she came rushing back with a bag of fish and chips, so hot it scalded her thigh through the thin plastic. She flopped onto the grass and unwrapped the pale paper. She inhaled the salty steam before offering the packet to Trân and Alana. For herself, Khalilah chose a golden fat chip, fried to a wrinkled brown at the edges. She dipped it into a tub of tangy tartar sauce. This was not the first time Khalilah had missed the new skateboard star's performance and she hated being told of the daring feats secondhand. She was also rather miffed Alana wasn't more interested. *Probably working on another mystery*, Khalilah grumbled to herself. *I wish she'd work on finding out who the skater is.*

"What's that?" Khalilah asked, looking over Alana's shoulder at the rounded, looped letters in Alana's notebook.

"Hmmm?" Alana mumbled. Alana wrote notes on whatever mystery she was working on, and this time it was Will and his family's startling resemblance to vampires. Thanks to Dr. Olivier's first homework assignment, Alana had drawn up a list of vampire characteristics and matched them to her observations. So far, she had eight.

1. Skin (too pale to be normal).
2. Unnatural grace.
3. Too skillful (i.e. ballroom dancing, violin).
4. Has raw beef for dinner (i.e. steak tartare).
5. No apparent appetite for "normal" food (i.e. canteen food).
6. Has an ability to connect with the spirit world.

7. Great Aunt Esme called the family "cursed."

8. Fangs!

Even with all the "evidence," Alana didn't feel confident about sharing her thoughts. She needed proof, and to get it required covert surveillance or, as Jefri would put it, a bit of good, old-fashioned backyard snooping. It couldn't be too hard. Her next door neighbor, Mrs. Whetu, did it all the time.

"Hooroo," Mrs. Whetu would say in her singsong voice, eyes darting about the edge of the door as soon as it opened, for a juicy titbit to describe to the gels. "The postman delivered your letters to my mailbox again. Just dropping them off."

Yeah, right, Alana thought. She was sure the nosy bat stole their mail on purpose and used a kettle and gloves before handing it back, resealed.

"I haven't seen your friend about for a while," Mrs. Whetu enquired archly, her nostrils working busily as if she could sniff Katriona out. "The one with the –"

"– wrinkles?" Alana offered helpfully.

"No, no..."

"– flat chest?"

"No, no..."

"– vestigial tail?"

"No, no..." Mrs. Whetu paused as she gave this image some thought. "Oh. Really?" she said. This was an unexpected, juicy titbit indeed!

Alana looked from side to side before leaning forward. Mrs. Whetu dropped her head in response. They were so close Alana could smell the cloying fog of Mrs. Whetu's stale potpourri perfume. Their two heads, one brown and one gray, formed a V. "She uses padding," Alana confided in a low voice, "to hide the tail."

Mrs. Whetu's eyebrows shot up but she realized she shouldn't be surprised. She'd heard about such things back in New Zealand. After all, a posterior that huge was hardly normal.

Alana continued. "But it's something she doesn't really like to talk about. You understand..."

Mrs. Whetu bobbed her head quickly. Even with

her eyes widened in shock, Alana was reminded of a rat. A rat who now thought Auntie Katriona had a tail! Oh it was wicked, there was no denying it. Alana could almost see Mrs. Whetu surrounded by the gels as she dropped her bombshell.

There was no reason Alana couldn't use the same strategy to do some spying on the new neighbors. And if she should get caught on the property she could always wave the mail, facepalm her forehead and say, "I've been looking for you. The postman delivered your letters to our mailbox by mistake..." And if they should look at her disbelievingly, she could say: "The postman does it all the time. Just ask my neighbor, Mrs. Whetu." And if they should drag her into the house, sink their fangs into her neck and suck her dry...?

It was a good thing Alana could run.

CHAPTER 24

Alive and kicking

"Running? You call that running?!"

At least Alana *thought* she could run. James disagreed. He didn't think much of anybody's fitness levels when he came to train Alana's soccer team, the Gibson Gibbons. When he'd last seen them – admittedly more than six months ago – the girls had been in top condition. They'd even beaten the Soccer Academy's Under-13s B-side, the BlueJay Bruisers. Now, for some reason, the girls were sloppy and distracted. James blamed himself. Work had kept him busy on overseas assignments for long periods of time. Although he still worked closely with Alana's mom, Emma, he shied away from the feelings of jealousy he'd experienced when her New Boyfriend had arrived on the scene. Without stopping to analyze why, this year James sought jobs that kept him abroad. But look at what had happened in his absence! The Blue-Jay Barbarians were sure to eat Alana and her friends alive!

Alana's soccer team, the Gibson Gibbons, was made up of Alana and Maddie, the twins, Prita and Preyasi, Khalilah in goal, and Sofia in reserve. Ordinarily, most of the girls were able to complete James's drills with ease, but today, only the twins could keep up. Alana hated to admit it, but without Coach Kusmuk and her punishing obstacle courses, most of them were not as fit as they used to be. And in the absence of a school field, weekly training in the shared gym with Coach McNeeson was simply not enough.

"Maybe if I didn't have to learn stupid twirls and balance books on my head, I'd be in better shape," Alana complained.

James blocked his ears at the flood of objections that followed. Gripes like, "restaurant overtime," "Grade 7 violin practice," and the "mystery skater" were swept away with an impatient wave.

"Excuses achieve nothing. Broun said that sweat

is the cologne of accomplishment, and by golly, I can't smell it yet," James grumbled at them. "We're doing it again."

Maddie aired the front of her shirt which had darkened from light blue to navy from perspiration. She waved her underarms. "You sure you can't smell it yet?" Maddie asked with a cheeky grin.

"Again!" James thundered.

In their down time, when they weren't training together but studying, rehearsing, and/or waiting tables, they texted each other about game plans and strategies and toyed with the idea of a new name for their team.

BFF ☺ ☺ ☺
Khalilah, Sofia, Maddie, Alana

Sofia:
How about "The Mighty Bombers?"

Alana:
Too much like a fighter pilot.
"Shockwave United?"

Khalilah:
Meh... "Lunatic Rockets?"

> **Maddie:**
> Too accurate. LOL. "Carnivore Chuckers?" Those girls were beefy.

> **Sofia:**
> Any takers for "Flying Monkeys?" or "Shaolin Bulls?"

> **Khalilah:**
> Or "Lightning Sharpshooters" because we're so deadly accurate with the ball.

But James was quick to reject the idea of a new team name. Fancy names weren't going to secure a win. You won the game because you trained hard and worked as a team. Today, James had a surprise for them. Desperate times called for desperate measures, he said. Soccer experts had agreed to help. The Gibson Gibbons stood in a loose arc, puffing from the 2-kilometer warm-up. They looked around for the soccer experts James was talking about. Apart from two kite-flyers, a tai-chi instructor, and a group of senior citizens, they saw no one.

"Gibson Gibbons, I'd like you to meet the Fairfield Falcons. Between them," James paused to wink, "they have hundreds of years of experience, and I hope for your sake, you'll be able to keep up."

Alana and the rest of the team exchanged disbelieving glances. *Keep up?* The five Falcons were geriatrics who made Mrs. Snell look like a teenager. There had to be some mistake.

"Um, no offense, James, but we can't play against *them*," Sofia said.

"Why not?" said one woman whose T-shirt claimed she was "Old but still kicking." "Scared?"

"Yeah, actually. Scared you'll need another hip replacement," Sofia said.

The older woman barked a laugh and made a big show of cracking her oversized knuckles. Arthritic bone mashed against arthritic bone. "We can look after ourselves. You just worry about messing up your pretty hair," and with that the five of them turned on their heel and jogged to the middle of the field.

As the knuckle-cracker – who they dubbed the General because she wore aviator sunglasses and talked with a large, unlit cigar in her mouth – took her team through their paces, the Gibson Gibbons looked at each of the women to assess their chances. Chuckles laughed at whatever anyone said. Hearing-Aid asked for everything to be repeated twice. Toothy kept adjusting her dentures, gave up, and shoved them in her pocket, and Goldilocks paid no attention at all as she reapplied her lipstick in "Popping Pink." Alana and her teammates exchanged rueful glances as they drew the same conclusion: Pushovers. To play soccer against these elderly nanas would be as cruel as clubbing baby seals. They'd best go easy on them.

"I'll keep it simple, Gibbons," said James. "Just get the ball," and with that he threw the soccer ball onto the ground. Chuckles took off with it with a deft flick of her foot. The Falcons became a blur of pastel cotton candy hair and wrinkles.

"Come on, Maddie," cried Sofia, who was marking Goldilocks.

"I'm trying," Maddie cried in frustration. The ball was not going very fast or very far, but Chuckles managed to block Maddie at every turn. She changed direction suddenly again and passed the ball to Toothy who shot it through Khalilah's legs and followed it down the field.

Khalilah looked through her legs, upside down. "Wow, she's good."

Alana had opted to sit it out to even up the numbers and couldn't believe Toothy had pulled a nutmeg on Khalilah. She jumped up and down from the sidelines and yelled encouragement. "Go, go, come on!"

Prita and Preyasi were onto it, but so was the General and Hearing-Aid, who between them kept the ball well away from the twins. It was like watching a game of cat-and-mouse. The Falcons toyed with them as the ball wove in and around the players, never quite within their grasp. By silent consensus, the Gibson Gibbons abandoned their Go Easy strategy and decided to Go All Out. But they didn't touch the ball once, not even after

Alana joined her team making it six (Gibbons) against five (Falcons).

Toothy was being tackled by Khalilah when her dentures fell out of her pocket and bounced off the ball. Khalilah took one look at the set of teeth sitting in their own puddle of saliva before squealing and running away. The older woman scooped up the offending item with a gappy grin and shunted the ball to Goldilocks, who headed the ball to the General with a grimace. While Goldilocks readjusted her hair, the General dribbled the ball toward Chuckles who was holding her sides from laughing at Goldilock's "hair" which had come off. She laughed even harder at Alana's attempts to tackle. Alana tried to elbow forward to gain some leverage but Chuckles shut her down with an inside-cut and swerved away, flipping the ball onto her knee in a move that was clearly just for show, before spinning around and kicking it away with her heel – *backward*!

"Congratulations, Lucy," James said to the General after forty minutes. "You've still got your magic! Thanks for coming in today, ladies. I know the girls learned a lot."

The Gibson Gibbons left after sheepishly shaking hands with the soccer matriarchs. There was a new respect in the girls' eyes and they slunk off the field with heads bowed, jerseys drooping around their shoulders to commiserate over the humiliating defeat. It was an emphatic lesson no one would forget in a hurry.

"Have they gone?" asked Lucy the General to Hearing-Aid. She stood ramrod straight, teeth chewing the end of her cigar with resolute ferocity.

"Are we on?" Hearing-Aid said.

"No! HAVE THEY GONE?" Lucy shouted.

"Who? The girls?" Chuckles asked, putting on her bifocals before checking behind the General's shoulder. "Yeah, they're gone."

"And James?"

"Yep."

The General crumpled at the announcement. She leant on Chuckles' arm as she massaged her hip. "I think I put my hip out again, darn it."

"Ooh, my knees!" Toothy groaned.

"That's the last time I'm listening to one of your crackpot ideas," complained Goldilocks, "hair" still askew.

"What?" said Hearing-Aid.

"I said, 'Never again,'" said Goldilocks loudly in Hearing-Aid's ear.

"Ohhh! Enjoy Phnom Penh!" Hearing-Aid nodded, shouting back. "But I don't think I'll be going anywhere." She stretched painfully. "I think I did my back in."

Goldilocks patted Hearing-Aid on the shoulder with a wry smile.

Then the Falcons limped off the field, fantasizing about bath salts and massages and being forty years younger.

CHAPTER 25

Still dead

It is time to look at the body again. You know you want to. It's only natural. To be curious. They say curiosity killed the cat but we both know that's not true. It was a python.

The first thing you'll notice about the body is that it has been turned over. Like a slice of meat that needs searing on both sides. It is such a little thing, this change in position, but it is a critical turning point – pardon the pun – because the first thing that hits you about the body is not its wide hips, or slight curve to the shoulders which suggest a stoop, but its hairstyle.

A bun.

Note, I said *bun*, not *buns*, so you can move your eyes up now.

The bun is white. It is as big and as round as an apple, now that it is no longer squashed against the coffee table surface. Like a Christmas ornament covered completely in snow.

Who *is* this person?

Well, she ain't no Sleeping Beauty, that's for sure.

CHAPTER 26

Pretty little lies

Soccer practice improved dramatically after their crushing defeat against the Falcons. The same, unfortunately, could not be said of Alana and Flynn's friendship which, according to Maddie, had reached subzero.

"*Brrrr*, it's not even winter yet, but I feel a definite cold snap," said Sofia, eyeing Flynn and Alana as they pointedly ignored each other during their free period. Flynn headed for the reference section, face averted, while Alana picked a random book on the table and pretended a sudden interest in sedimentary rocks.

"Yeah," agreed Khalilah through her raspberry specs, "I think it's what you call a '*micro*climate.'"

"Well, she sure is cute and little," Maddie agreed with a smirk, patting Alana's head which was now considerably lower than her own. Alana growled.

"Uh-oh," Sofia said, placing a warning hand on Maddie's arm, "I'm sensing a storm front."

Alana pointedly ignored her friends as she read the paragraph on "lithification" for the third time. She wondered what Flynn was doing here, and whether he was still mad at her. Around the corner from where Alana sat, Flynn was looking blankly at a book on entomology ... written in Spanish.

"G'day, Mate! Or should I say, hola amigo?" Jefri said to Flynn after a quick glance at the heavy volume in Flynn's hands.

"Oh, hey, Jefri," Flynn said glumly, replacing the reference book on the shelf.

"Call me wacko but you don't look like a happy little Vegemite," Jefri said. "What's up, Possum?"

Flynn looked at Jefri's gentle face and felt an inexplicable urge to confide in him. Half the time he had no idea what Jefri was talking about, but Flynn knew the boy's heart was in the right place.

"I just don't get some people, y'know? One day they act like they're your friend and then maybe even more than a friend, and then you find out they think you're completely lame, and it's... I dunno..." Flynn's eyes were drawn to where Alana sat reading as he trailed off.

Jefri followed his gaze and a look of understanding entered his eyes. Khalilah had told him of the on-again, off-again relationship between her two friends. "Leave it with me, Possum," and before Flynn could do or say anything to stop him, Jefri walked over to his sister and her friends.

"Hey Alana," he whispered loudly, "Flynn was thinking of chucking a sickie and wanted to know if you were up for it."

"Who, Alana? Ditch class? Are you crazy?" Khalilah asked, shaking her head in disbelief.

"I'm being fair dinkum, completely true blue," Jefri held his hand up like a scout.

"This is *Alana* we're talking about, the scholarship student and don't-touch-my-books-because-they're-in-alphabetical-order-psycho-chick," Maddie explained to Jefri patiently.

But Alana was already gathering her things.

Maybe Flynn had forgiven her, or was at least willing to listen to an apology. Either way, she wasn't going to miss this opportunity. Sofia was quick to pick up on her friend's feelings. She'd always suspected there was the possibility of romance for Alana and Flynn and now here was a chance. Alice may have created a wedge between them, but Sofia was confident Alana and Flynn could get back on track. Which is why, she explained later, she kicked Alana's chair from under her.

"What th-?!" Alana spluttered from the library floor.

"You can thank me later," Sofia said in Alana's ear as she helped her sit up.

Jefri was already dragging Flynn to the scene. "Holy dooley, Flynn! You have to take Alana to see Nurse Cathy! It looks like she's come a cropper!"

Alana gave a start. Skipping class so she could explain herself to Flynn was one thing. Voluntarily visiting the clinic was something else. "It's not that bad, I'm fine. Oww!" she yelled, glaring at Sofia.

Sofia removed her foot from Alana's fingers.

"Stop being so proud, Alana," she admonished. Sofia looked at Flynn with a roll of her eyes that said: She is *so* stubborn.

Flynn looked around the table.

"Sorry, I can't take her." Maddie said, finally cottoning on. "I've got violin."

"Don't look at me," said Sofia, "Miller and I are working on the Fibonacci sequence. Woohoo! #Fibonacci totes epic! Right, Miller?" she called out to Miller across the room with a pump of her arm. Miller looked both confused and excited.

Flynn looked at Khalilah who shook her head with regret. "I'm sorry Flynn. I've got Malay."

Flynn's eyes narrowed. "Huh? I thought you *were* Malay?"

Jefri cut in. "She means we have Malay *tutoring*." When Flynn looked unconvinced, Jefri shrugged. "What can I say? We're a pair of dags."

"Hey, speak for yourself!" Khalilah exclaimed.

"Quickly! You's better nick off before someone catches you bludging," Jefri warned, and it was no idle threat. Already the librarian could be heard stomping in their direction.

As soon as the pair had gone, Jefri's face slipped into an easy grin. "My oath, but I'm good!"

Khalilah shook her head as she exchanged incredulous glances with Maddie and Sofia. "My brother a matchmaker? Now I've seen everything!"

CHAPTER 27

A change of heart

Alana refused to go to the clinic so she convinced Flynn they could wait it out until their next class, in one of the inner gardens. Alana knew she had to explain what had happened with Alice but she didn't know where to start. At least not without having to also explain *why*.

"Coltrane isn't too bad," Alana offered to the silence that had settled between them.

Flynn raised an eyebrow. "Not too bad?"

"Okay, he's pretty amazing," she conceded.

Flynn gestured with his hand to draw higher praise from Alana, praise that he knew had to come.

"Alright, alright, Coltrane is incredible," Alana sighed, as if the admission was akin to a tooth extraction.

Flynn nudged her shoulder. "Yeah, he *is*."

The strident sound of the bell signaled the start

of their next class. Even though Flynn and Alana made their way to the Police Boys' Club slowly, they were still the first ones to arrive. Alana felt tongue-tied and awkward. Although she couldn't stand ballroom dancing, Alana was almost looking forward to Will's icy touch. Perhaps it could cool Alana's cheeks which she knew were blazing brighter than a bushfire. But even that hope was dashed when Mrs. Cronenberg announced a change of partners.

"You and you," she said, pushing two students together, "and you and you," she continued. On and on down the line until only Alana, Khalilah, Miller, and Flynn were left. "Hmmm," Mrs. Cronenberg said thoughtfully. A mental eenie, meenie, minie, mo made her eyes flick from one to the other. Alana stared at her feet. Flynn stared at Alana, while Khalilah stared at Mrs. Cronenberg's towering headpiece. Today it was a mountain of brightly colored fruit, donuts, and iced confections. Mrs. Cronenberg shot Khalilah a nervous glance before pairing Alana with Miller.

Alana breathed a silent prayer of thanks a minute too soon. "No, no. On second thought..." With a satisfied nod, she replaced Alana's trembling hand within Flynn's instead.

Mrs. Cronenberg's voluminous skirts swept away and the familiar strains of the waltz began. Alana crushed Flynn's foot under a heavy black boot with her first step.

"Sorry," she mumbled.

"No, my fault," Flynn said, a hint of a smile in his voice, "I was too slow."

They began again, this time Flynn deftly slipping his feet from under Alana's before she had time to squash them. It was not the waltz. It looked more like a game of *Snap* played with feet where neither opponent wanted to win.

"Relax," Flynn urged, shaking Alana's hand lightly in his.

But relaxing wasn't something Alana could do. Her mouth felt like the Sahara Desert and all her body fluids seemed to have migrated to her underarms. How did Mrs. Cronenberg expect Alana to count time, move gracefully, remember the steps, *and* not throw up on everyone's shoes?

Alana looked around the room wildly. Khalilah and Miller were stepping neatly, if not a bit woodenly, in a square. Maddie and Jefri had given up on the waltz and were doing a bush dance whenever Mrs. Cronenberg wasn't looking, and Sofia and Will were dancing cheek-to-cheek. Alana saw a flash of white. Was that a *fang* emerging from Will's mouth? She stumbled forward in a panic and smashed into Sofia and Will who were jolted apart.

"Are you okay, Alana?" Flynn asked, concerned.

Alana craned her neck to check on Sofia. Both she and Will had resumed dancing, this time a respectable distance apart. Alana breathed a sigh of relief. "Je suis très bien," she said automatically, lapsing into French as they had done over the summer. I'm fine. Alana looked Flynn in the eye. "Je suis désolé." I'm sorry. Somehow saying sorry in French was so much easier than saying it in

English. "For all that stuff I said to Alice, before. None of it was true."

Flynn pulled her out of the way as Maddie and Jefri do-si-doed past, bringing their bodies even closer. "So if John Coltrane is incredible, what does that make me?" he asked.

"Conceited," Alana shot back, a twinkle in her eye.

Flynn squeezed her hand and held it, even after the music had stopped and it was time to go. The pair of them grinned goofily at each other, and then Alana smiled into her chest. Maybe everything was going to be okay.

Khalilah's head appeared between Flynn and Alana's. "Call me a ding bat, but I reckon we're in for a heatwave." Khalilah fanned Alana's flushed face with her hand and beamed.

"You see," protested Jefri, "you *do* talk like that, here," to which Khalilah left the amused pair to chase her brother.

"They're just movies! None of it is real!"

CHAPTER 28

A night to remember

Alana and her friends decided to celebrate the end-of-first-term break with a trip to the movies. In light of Dr. Olivier's English and drama class, everybody was keen to go to the Pan-Asian Short Film Festival at the local arthaus theater, The Dendy, especially as this year's theme was horror. At least everybody started out keen, until one by one, they bailed.

"Mom says we're completely booked out. She said I can go, but I know they'll find it hard to do it without me..." Sofia moaned.

Alana gave her friend a hug. "I'll help, too," she offered.

"No," Sofia protested. "It's okay. Miller's already coming. Plus, I need you to tell me what happens." Alana shook her head in dismay. Sofia routinely read the ending of books first and sought out "spoiler alerts."

Khalilah and Jefri were the next to cancel. Alana could barely recognize her friend's voice on the phone. "Jefri hath pathed on hith thtupid cold," Khalilah croaked down the line, congested. "Perfect timing for the holidayth!" She sounded bitterly disappointed. Horror movies were her favorite. Especially the ones filmed in Thailand, which were so over the top, they were really comedies.

"Shall I drop over? Do you need anything? Cough drops? Chicken soup?" Alana said, concerned. The sound of violent hacking in the background muffled Khalilah's reply.

"Arghh! Thtop coughing on me! You're thpreading your germth everywhere," Alana heard Khalilah scold. "Don't come over! Thethe germth are lethal," Khalilah warned. "Muuum! Abang, ith thtealing my cream bun!" Khalilah yelled. "Thorry, Lana, gotta go," and after a wet splutter in Alana's ear, she was gone.

Alana was already waiting outside the cinema when Maddie's text message came through.

"Babysittg. Rainchk. 4giv me?"

"Yeah, right," Alana muttered. Maddie was most likely practicing for the orchestra auditions which were coming up soon. If she'd really wanted to come tonight, there were any number of aunts, uncles and cousins she could have called on for help.

Which just left...

"Flynn! Hi!" Alana's stomach performed a familiar triple somersault at the sight of him. Jeans hugged his lanky frame and a plain black T-shirt, once baggy, now clung to his form – Flynn had filled out considerably over the summer. He smiled a greeting and ran impatient fingers through his unruly mop of hair. Alana's hands itched to pull it back from his face so she could see his eyes. She wondered what kind of gray they were tonight. Stormy, with a hint of purple? Or slate with a tinge of blue? She remembered, vaguely, a time when she thought Flynn was nothing but an unkempt slob. Alana dropped her eyes. Things seemed very different now. Alana rubbed her hands down the leg of her own jeans and plucked nervously at her favorite Jimi Hendrix T-shirt – a birthday present from her friends, last year. "It looks like it's just you and me," she apologized in a rush. "Sofia and Miller are working at Brothers, Khalilah and Jefri are down with a cold, and ..."

"C'est parfait!" That's perfect, he said in French, before enveloping her hand easily within his own, tugging her toward the growing line where they waited in line to buy their tickets. He made holding hands feel simple. Normal. As natural as breathing air... just before an asthma attack. Alana felt her palms become slick with sweat and her chest felt tight. Was her tongue swelling? It felt massive. Like it was overtaking her mouth and filling her throat. Maybe she had caught Khalilah's cold? She should check. Bathroom. Mirrors had bathrooms. No, that wasn't right. Oh crud. What if she choked on her own tongue? How embarrassing would that be?

Alana.

Without any warning, Alana heard her dad's voice. She resisted the urge to turn around. She knew he wasn't really here. Hadn't she heard him hundreds of times before? Usually before she was about to do something daunting. Always reassuring Alana that she could do this. That she had it In The Bag. That everything was going to be alright.

Alana and her dad used to play a game when she was little, a game where Hugo would make Alana choose whatever superpower she needed to conquer her fear. Gills for breathing underwater when she used the diving board for the first time, stretchable toes which kept her balanced on her bike...

Help, she thought, *what kind of superpower do I need now?*

Just then Flynn's hand gave a tiny tremble. Alana looked up and realized with a jolt that Flynn was just as nervous as she was. Gone was the cocky slouch, the carefree grin. Flynn looked shy, and kind of pleading, and maybe even a bit, well... *scared.*

Maybe the sweat pooling between their palms didn't belong to her. Maybe the jerky gasps weren't only coming from her throat. Maybe she didn't need a superpower because she was already powerful. Look at what she'd done to Flynn! Alana felt her breathing slow and her body flood with... with what? With something that felt like calm and adrenaline at the same time. Something like what she imagined The Force must feel like. That was it. The Force was with her. And her dad. And he *did* approve.

He was right.

She could do this.

...

"No, no, no, the worst bit was when the mummy came out of the closet and unraveled herself to strangle him with her bandages!" said Alana.

"How can you say that? It had to be when the

zombie ripped off the doll's head with his mouth and started choking..." argued Flynn.

"Or the shower scene. That was pretty funny, too. Kind of like Hitchcock meets Tarantino..."

"... meets Jackie Chan..."

Alana gave an unexpected chortle which made her drink spurt through her nostrils. Flynn doubled-up, clutched his sides and backed away, laughing.

"Gross! That is so gross!"

Alana clutched her nose in pain. The effervescent bubbles were agony but she couldn't stop laughing. She felt drunk on happiness. Most of the movie-goers had already drifted away to argue the merits of the films over coffee. Pockets of people spilled out of surrounding cafés onto the pavement, like bobbing flotsam from a ship. Alana's phone buzzed. It was James. He'd sent a video of what looked like soccer moves from the World Cup archives, which she would have checked instantly... any other time. Alana didn't give herself time to think why tonight was different and pocketed her phone. She glanced at her watch.

"I'd better go," she said, pulling away reluctantly. "It's late. I had a great time, though."

Flynn's eyes mirrored her disappointment, but he was quick to disguise it. "Me too. Apart from the 'drink thing.' Which was almost scarier than the horror films. Like, it could have been made into a movie of its own. They could call it, 'Attack of the Schnoz.'"

Alana thumped his arm but without any real venom. That was another weird thing she found herself doing. Hitting Flynn. Punching him. Pushing him. Not that her hands made much impact. His body was rock-hard. It must be all those exercises Flynn did at the barre: pliés, and jetés, or whatever they called them, in ballet. He was asking for it, anyway. Comments like that. It was his own fault.

Flynn rubbed his arm in mock hurt. "You punch like a girl."

"You dress like a busker," she shot back.

As if on cue, a busker behind them started

drumming. If you could call "drumming" banging the top of two metal trashcans with drumsticks, and the side of two upside-down bins. They turned.

Bang. Bing. Bang. Bing. Boom. Ka-thud. Boom.

The jarring sounds seemed to hold the squat man in a trance. He shook his head from side-to-side in time with the beat with his eyes closed. Flynn, who played the saxophone, shuddered at the lack of musicality. But that wasn't the worst of it. The beanie on top of the man's head threatened to shoot off into the air because it was three sizes too small. A woolly waistcoat cuddled the man's rounded belly, and the threadbare shorts he wore had rips in all the wrong places. Tartan socks within fake Doc Marten's tapped a rhythm of their own. Flynn was silently horrified. He dressed in a casual, off-beat way on purpose. The busker looked like he'd closed his eyes before reaching into the cupboard... at the Goodwill Shop. Alana was comparing Flynn to *this guy?*

"You dance like an elephant," Flynn retaliated.

Alana's fists flailed at Flynn's chest. "No, I don't. I'm worse," she admitted. "I'm like an elephant that's been shot with a dart gun in its last death throes..."

"... on a good day," said Flynn, catching her fists, locking them to him.

Alana fell silent. If she fanned her fingers out, she still wouldn't be able to reach his chest from end to end. "That's a low blow, Flynn Tucker. I can't help it if I've got two left feet."

Flynn opened her fists. They succumbed to the gentle pressure easily. "Hey bro, can you do three-four timing?" Flynn yelled over his shoulder.

The busker, after several attempts, managed a stuttering beat. Despite Alana's embarrassed attempts to pull away, Flynn began to guide her through the waltz. "Give it up, Oakley," he said into her ear, "you're going to conquer the waltz and I'm going to help you."

Some onlookers laughed. Others cheered. A few of them clapped. Emboldened, the busker beat his trashcans and lids louder. One couple began to dance alongside them. And then another. And another. It was ten o'clock on a Friday night in May on King Street and the pavement was full of waltzing couples. Newtown had seen dog shows, knitting on trees and kooky costumes, but it had never seen anything like this. Passing cars beeped their horns in approval as they passed.

"You are IN-SANE, Tucker," Alana said, with a disbelieving shake of her head.

Flynn shrugged. "And *you* are waltzing, Oakley."

Alana looked down at her feet and promptly tripped.

"Don't think. Just let yourself go. Trust me. I've got you," Flynn said.

Alana looked back up and fell into Flynn's eyes. They weren't stormy with a hint of purple. Or slate with a tinge of blue. Flynn's eyes were warm and dark like a pebble baking in the hot sun.

You could lose yourself in eyes like that. You could trust them. You could let go.

So she did.

CHAPTER 29

Gross but cool

Flynn turned on his side and cupped his face to stare at Alana. They were lying in a spot in the park which was shaded and grassy, somewhere where they were unlikely to be hit by a Frisbee or football. He was careful not to dislodge the earbud from his ear because he wanted to take in the music as he watched. Flynn and Alana were listening to Jeff Buckley. It was on Alana's pen drive of songs which she'd finally given to Flynn, her own mixed tape version of P.J. Harvey, Janis Joplin, and AC/DC. Of the songs Flynn had given her, Alana said she loved John Coltrane and David Bowie, but was less than impressed with Tom Waits. She understood him as a musician, she said, but not as a vocalist. He made everything sound like a suicide note, or creepy, or worse, like a creepy suicide note. Flynn liked how Alana didn't care she was committing sacrilege. Alana had never been afraid to disagree with him and these days, wasn't afraid to agree with him, either.

Alana looked even smaller when she was lying down. Her dark hair fanned out like it was floating in the sea and her eyes bunched shut like she was just about to blow out birthday candles. She was concentrating on the lyrics and mouthing the words. All trace of her cute dimples was gone.

Flynn loved to watch her lips move.

Flynn loved to watch her lips.

Flynn loved to watch her.

...

Alana listened to Jeff Buckley crooning in her ear as she sang along and snuck a look at Flynn from beneath her lashes. From this angle she could see his lips which were parted, just enough so that they made a tiny "O." They looked soft. Alana imagined biting into them. She wondered if that made her as bad as a vampire. Or worse.

Alana's eyes closed and then fluttered open on impulse, so that she saw it happen before she felt it. Wet. And warm. She wiped her mouth with the back of her hand and sat up so suddenly Flynn and Alana almost knocked heads.

"I can*not* believe you did that!" Alana shouted.

"I... it..." Mortification painted Flynn's face a deep red. "It just happened. I couldn't help it."

"You *dribbled* on me. What are you? Two?!"

"Think of it as drooling for you," Flynn joked weakly.

"Either way, it's gross," Alana said, lying back down with her arms crossed, clamping down on the smile that threatened to split her face wide open. She hugged the thought to her heart, hard. She made Flynn Tucker drool. How cool was that?

Gross.

But cool.

CHAPTER 30

A close shave

Thwuck! The knife whistled through the air and landed near Jefri's trembling elbow.

"Strewth, that was a bit close!" he protested.

Khalilah rubbed her hands together. "That was only my warm-up," she said. "I think I can do better."

Alana picked up a knife and bent it backward and forward. They were made from rubber, similar to the props used in movies. Alana was teaching Flynn something, this time: knife-throwing for learning the waltz. It felt like a fair exchange.

"Have a go," Alana said, stretching out to give Flynn the knife. But Khalilah grabbed it before he could.

"Let me have another go, first," Khalilah said grimly.

"I already said I was sorry, Possum," Jefri whined. "No need to chuck a wobbly."

Chapter 30

"I missed most of the school holidays because of you," Khalilah said. *Thwuck*. "And I missed soccer practice." *Thwuck*. "And the movies." *Thwuck*. "AND the Bondi Beach Skate Bowl." *Thwuck*. *Thwuck*. *Thwuck*.

Jefri yelped. Each knife landed in quick succession near both of his ears, neck, and hips. There were two knives remaining. Alana snatched them from the table just in time. Khalilah's eyes looked murderous.

"Let's give Flynn a turn, shall we?" Alana suggested.

Khalilah got out of the way in a huff. Alana demonstrated the throwing action in slow motion. She handed Flynn the knife and adjusted his stance and the position of his shoulders. She had to reach up on tip-toes to do so. Alana felt momentarily miffed that everybody else was growth spurting and leaving her behind. At this rate, she might never grow again! What if she ended up the same height as Coach Kusmuk? Alana suppressed a shudder.

Flynn did some practice leg squats and then ran on the spot. "Don't worry," he called out with confidence, then instructed, "Just don't move." Flynn leaned back and stretched his arm as far as he could. With a grunt, he released the blade with an overarm pitch that reminded Alana of a drunken cricket bowler.

Thwuck-k-k-k! The knife wobbled in place. Jefri looked down. He couldn't have moved even if he'd tried. Flynn had him pinned to the target by his baggy crotch.

"Oi! That's my Down Under!" Jefri squeaked.

Flynn held up apologetic hands. "Sorry, Jefri. I was aiming above your head."

Jefri found no comfort in the news.

Khalilah held out the final knife to Flynn. "Why don't you take another shot?" she said sweetly.

CHAPTER 31

Snooping, shopping, and an epiphany

With her friendship-or-something-more with Flynn back on track, Alana had one thing left to accomplish before school started: to gather more "intel" on Will and his family. Since their day at the beach, Alana had discovered another fact to add to her list of suspicions: Will's mother had a clothing store on the south end of King Street called Revamped. It turns out she was a dab hand at upcycling fashion from old clothes, and her newly acquired fans – Sofia, Maddie, and Khalilah – were the perfect excuse to drop in and do some snooping. The first thing Alana noticed was that the shop's interior was decorated in much the same way as the family home, an eclectic mix of antiques and original new-from-old items.

"I love this style," enthused Maddie, on one

of her rare breaks from violin practice. "It's so Steampunk!"

"This is Steampunk?" Alana said, surprised. Alana looked at the décor with new eyes. *Doesn't change anything, though*, she thought stubbornly. *All the other weird stuff about Will still holds.*

"Thanks," Will's mother, Corinne Löfgren, answered. "Will made those. He's like me. Will likes to tinker with old junk and make it into something new, only I prefer fabric."

"And your husband prefers dead animals," said Alana under her breath.

"Your son is a really amazing dancer," Sofia ventured to say shyly.

Corinne shook a head of red-gold curls. She had the same pale skin of her children with an almost porcelain sheen, and light brown eyes that were strangely reflective. Corinne was dressed in one of her own creations – a wraparound dress to which she had added long, bat-like sleeves with an accordion fold. "I used to work in theater, costume design and the like, and of course the performers would look after the children, from time to time, to keep them from getting under my feet. An elderly couple, the Schiapelli's, taught Will ballroom dancing." She chuckled. "I still remember him riding the tops of Mrs. Schiapelli's shoes when he was three years old, dressed in a tuxedo I'd made for him."

Dancing since he was three?

"And of course, Alice was glued to the violin by the same age. Martin made sure of that. Terrible actor, but a brilliant musician," Corinne reflected.

"No wonder Alice is so incredible," Maddie interjected. "I've never seen anyone play the violin like her."

"Yes," Alana couldn't resist adding snidely, "your family is certainly unique."

If Corinne noticed the tone in Alana's voice, she ignored it, preferring instead to reassure Maddie that Alice couldn't help it. "Alice has Ehlers-Danlos syndrome. Her body doesn't produce much collagen which gives her almost circus flexibility," she explained to the girls' puzzled glances. "The upside is that it gives her a physical advantage when she plays the violin. Her hands are extremely flexible. But the downside is muscle fatigue, weak lungs, and easily damaged skin. She has to be careful not to overdo it."

"Wasn't there a famous violinist with the same thing?" said Sofia slowly, dredging her memory of random trivia. "People accused him of having made a deal with the devil because he played so well."

"Ah yes," Corinne smiled, "Niccolò Paganini: a man who supposedly exchanged his immortal soul for exceptional musical talent."

"Paganini?" Maddie exclaimed excitedly. "He was the world's greatest violinist!" she said. "They say he could play up to a thousand notes a minute, and could double- and triple-stop. That means play multiple notes at once," Maddie explained in a rush, "and even do *left-handed pizzicato*!"

Sofia and Alana, who didn't know Maddie was describing a plucking technique that usually used the non-bowing hand – hence the excitement – nodded with vague interest, while Khalilah, who thought *pizza* was involved, showed more enthusiasm.

A tiny part of Maddie felt crushed that Alice shared the same physical characteristics as her idol and not for the first time, she experienced a spiky heat that blew hot and cold at once. Alice was everywhere she turned – with her perfect trills, deeply moving vibratos, and screechy laugh that made Maddie's ears shed skin like a cheese grater. She wondered if it was wrong to fantasize about the younger girl being squeezed by an anaconda and then squashed flat by a falling piano. Then Maddie realized with dismay that she was jealous. It felt strange on her tongue. It had a kind of vomit-like sourness that made her mouth pucker. But just as quickly Maddie realized the physical cost: muscle fatigue, weak lungs, and easily damaged skin. Late nights at the movies for Alice were unlikely. She could never try out for the Gibson Gibbons. Alice would never be able to sunbake at Bondi Beach with friends.

Friends.

Maddie realized with a start that she had spent so much of her time obsessing about Being The Best that she'd neglected her own friends. And they, in turn, had stopped including her in their plans. Why bother when they knew the answer was going to be no? Maddie couldn't even remember the last time she'd taken an interest in what her friends were doing – too busy urging them to listen to her audition pieces. Something they were doing with less and less enthusiasm.

What did you get when you put nothing into a relationship? When the "Me" and the "I want" outweighed everything and everyone else? When reaching a goal and ambition became more important than friendship?

An audience.

You had to be careful what you wished for.

...

Alana noticed with regret that her vampire theories were fast unraveling as Corinne chatted and flitted around the store, holding up prospective outfits against each of the girls' frames. *Will's dad, Vlad, comes from Sweden and my family is from Ireland, so we suffer terribly from sunburn and avoid the outdoors wherever possible. I'm sure that's why we've all got such terrible circulation, and of course Alice's skin is so delicate. Ooh, I like this color on you, Maddie. Steak tartare tastes wonderful! We often eat food raw. So many nutrients are lost after cooking. How about this, Sofia? This has a real boho-chic feel to it. Have the children still got that silly game? Will's always messing around. I'm sorry if he scared you. Try this scarf, Khalilah. It's really cute with the bear ears sewn on.*

Alana was losing patience. With her theory in shreds, all she had left was a creepy great aunt and fangs. At least it wasn't a creepy great aunt *with* fangs.

Or not that she'd noticed...

"What does your husband do, Mrs. Löfgren?" Alana asked, knowing she was grasping at straws.

"My husband? Vlad?" Corinne repeated, for once at a loss. She stared out the shop window where pedestrians were rushing past to escape a sudden downpour. The image reminded Alana of a Monet painting – soft and slightly out of focus. A whiplash of lightning illuminated the darkened street and as if on cue, Will and Alice suddenly appeared on either side of their mother. Their presence was almost menacing and Corinne seemed to fold in on herself as she shrank toward the rack of clothes behind her.

"You don't want to know about Dad," said Will with a meaningful look at his mother.

Alice advanced from the other side and agreed. "Dad is very, very boring. Isn't he, Mom?"

Alana raised an eyebrow. Corinne had burrowed into the Specials Rack. "Yes, dears. Very, very boring," she squeaked, eyes downcast, picking at her hem.

As soon as there was a break from the rain, the girls said goodbye and left the warm interior, only to be embraced by a bitter wind. Each gust hinted at the bite of winter to come. Khalilah was thankful for her new scarf with the bear ears, which she wrapped more tightly around her neck. Alana followed suit as she pulled on a second beanie and tagged along with her friends to a nearby café for lunch. The reconnaissance mission had yielded an intriguing lead – Will and Alice had been too keen to convince them that their dad was "very, very boring" and Alana was determined to find out why.

CHAPTER 32

Your own worst enemy

"A disappointing effort, Miss Oakley," Mrs. Snell tutted as she handed Alana back her essay on *Reel History: A look at the history of horror films.* "I expect more from you."

Alana fared no better in English and even worse in math. "Is everything okay at home?" Mr. Hornby felt compelled to ask, to which Alana could only shake her head in embarrassment. The only subject she wasn't failing was science, but that was because Miss Metcalf let the students do whatever they want so she could check the surf scene on her computer. Last class some students worked on the physics' principle of Hooke's Law with a pogo stick, while others experimented with rocket-making outside. People were either bouncing and falling all over class or running from falling debris.

Alana knew her lack of concentration was

affecting her work. She also knew how to fix it. But knowing it and doing it were two very different things.

"You hang up first," Alana whispered, looking at the clock. The digital display by her bed said 11:05.

"No, you hang up," Flynn said.

Twenty minutes of silence later...

"Hang up the phone, Flynn."

"I will after you do it."

The late-night calls had to stop. Hours of listening to each other just breathe. Alana wondered if it was weird that that was all they wanted to do. That it *physically hurt* to disconnect the phone.

"You can borrow my glasses if you like," Khalilah offered one day while they were studying Malay at her home. Mr. and Mrs. Madzaini were inordinately pleased with Khalilah's academic progress, which they attributed to the red resin frames. Khalilah balanced her glasses on Alana's nose. "See, you look smarter already."

What nobody realized was that Khalilah was transforming study, especially the periodic table, into a format she could understand. The molecule for water (H_2O) for example, was the girl Oxygen, towing the twin Hydrogens from her plaits. And Fluorine had anger issues because it was the most reactive chemical element. A glance at her science notebook could easily have been mistaken for a modern interpretation of Tolstoy's *War and Peace*... but with weirder names.

Sadly, there was no such breakthrough in learning for Alana no matter how much more intelligent she looked in specs. The situation got so dire that after the third week back at school, Alana was called into the deputy principal's office. To Mr. Turner's annoyance, Alana was unable to offer a satisfactory explanation for her falling grades.

"The Sir Marcus Oliphant Scholarship is awarded to the student who best displays temerity, curiosity, and intelligence, as well as a high standard of physical competence. Lately your academic record has been sorely lacking in all three, and you're barely scraping a Pass in P.E. If this continues..."

Alana nodded her head. She understood the consequences. Flynn or no Flynn, it was time for her to Pull Up Her Socks or else.

CHAPTER 33

Prisoner of love

Soccer training, school assignments, and the looming mid-year exams made time pass in a blur. The four girls took turns hosting revision weekends to prepare. Alana made a determined effort to work harder after the talk with Mr. Turner, but Sofia couldn't resist bringing the vampire trilogy along and took to reading a few pages from them aloud. The other girls often stopped what they were doing to listen to her. At this, adults of the household always shook their heads and muttered about "fairy-tale nonsense" and "unrealistic expectations."

"They puke, they snore, they fart," Auntie Mo of the Dawson household said, glowering at Uncle Joe who released a loud belch. "The sooner you realize it, the better!" This last sentence, Alana felt, was directed at little Cassy, who lay in the same makeshift bed of flowers made months before.

Her tiny, button nose buried in the same story.

"Being a princess isn't all it's cracked up to be, you know," Khalilah said to Cassy. "I should know," she muttered.

But the girls didn't care none of it was real. They knew boys didn't really glitter in the sun, or were too hot to wear shirts in the middle of winter. Love wasn't logical. "Do you think we'll ever find love like that?" was their favorite question.

Everyone scoffed except Emma.

"Oh yes," she insisted. "I found Alana's dad, Hugo," cupping her head dreamily in one hand as she stirred her coffee with a pen.

Alana sighed and swapped the pen for a teaspoon. She wanted to believe in the kind of love her parents had shared, but would she ever find it? How would she know it was real and not some corny high school infatuation? *And which is Flynn?* The question snuck into her head and pitched a camping spot.

Alana made an effort to refocus. "Can someone test me on history?"

Sofia fixed her ear buds firmly into place and turned up the volume on Jet Tierbert. She did *not* want to listen to all the creative ways a person could be tortured or killed.

"Name the animal whose skin toxins are used to coat blowpipe darts by the Columbian Indians of the Embera Choco region," said Maddie.

"*Phyllobates terribilis* or the Golden Poison Frog. Its common name is 'Poison Dart Frog,' or *kokoi* in the local language."

Maddie smiled. "Correct. An adult terribilis contains around one milligram of poison which is enough to kill one human, between one and ten humans, or between ten to twenty humans?"

"Between ten to twenty."

"Yep."

While Alana and Maddie continued to test each other on poisons like tetrodotoxin – a toxin so deadly it was 1,200 times more poisonous than cyanide – Khalilah jumped up and seized Sofia by the hands. She began to swing her around in a circle, humming the waltz.

"What are you doing?" Sofia cried, giggling.

Maddie jumped up to join them. Sofia began to dance with Maddie, as Khalilah grabbed Mrs. Oakley. Round and round they twirled. Emma laughed good-naturedly as they spun. Their humming turned into lahs.

"*Lah, lah, lah.* Come on, Alana," Maddie said, reaching out her hand. But Alana refused to join in. "The chemical formula of Batrachotoxin is $C_{31}H_{42}N_2O_6$," she said loudly, eyes screwed shut.

"What's wrong with Alana?" Emma wanted to know.

"Cinderella's grumpy because she's too young to go to the ball," Sofia said with a mischievous grin.

"The ball?"

"The Year Ten formal," Khalilah explained, puffing slightly from the twirl.

"Yep," Maddie said. "We've been learning Ballroom Dancing and Alana would LOVE to show off her new dance moves but only Year Tens get to go." She dodged a cushion. "Mrs.

Cronenberg –"

"– our dance teacher –" Khalilah explained, ducking.

"– thinks Alana is very special." The girls giggled as another cushion sailed past.

Alana ran out of cushions to throw. "Mrs. Cronenberg can drop dead for all I care! There is no way I'm doing the waltz and I wish she'd get out of my life."

"The waltz is lovely, Alana, but I guess it *is* a bit old-fashioned. Shall I show you girls the dancing I liked to do when I was your age? It was retro even when I was young, though," Emma said apologetically. Despite Alana's protests that nobody wanted to see Emma Shake Her Booty, Emma proceeded to do so, leading the four girls in lots of finger jabbing at the ceiling.

"Don't stop 'til you get enough," Emma sang.

All four girls promptly sat down.

CHAPTER 34

Kusmuk finds her banana

Alana and her friends turned up for Ballroom Dancing with the rest of her class on Monday morning to find a note taped to the door:

❧

Ballroom Dancing is canceled
until further notice ❧

Alana felt a surge of elation. They heard the *boom boom boom* of a beatboxer well before they saw Trân leading a small group of Second-Chancers. He was heading their way. Khalilah *whooped*. There was no doubt in her mind that Trân was replacing Mrs. Cronenberg to teach them some "old-school moves," a bit of breakdancing, moonwalking, maybe even a bit of head spinning. Trân spotted them too and beatboxed a greeting:

It's Hotchickalana,
Hangin' out with Khalilah.
So nice to see ya'

They ride boards with no feah-ya!

While Alana was not as excited as Khalilah, she still felt a sense of relief. She didn't care what moves Trần had in mind, as long as it didn't involve someone invading her personal space. *Even if that someone is Flynn?* A voice in her head asked. Alana ignored the slight pang of regret and raised her hand to slap Khalilah's in a high five. Only it wasn't Khalilah's hand that clamped onto hers. This hand was much smaller with the strength of a Rottweiler's jaws.

"Nice to see you, too, Oakley," Coach Kusmuk grinned before twisting Alana's hand up and then behind her back, before flipping her over. Alana found herself face-to-face with the ceiling.

Coach Kusmuk's voice wiped the triumph from Khalilah's face. "Welcome to martial arts! In this class we will be learning specific skills from judo, jujitsu, karate, aikido, tae kwon do, and hapkido. Each of these self-defense techniques requires a great deal of strength, coordination, and agility, but none of this will help you if your mind is weak," Kusmuk announced, indicating Alana on the floor, "as my volunteer has demonstrated."

The group moved to the mats in the great hall. Khalilah waved forlornly at Trần as he disappeared into the dance studio. Kusmuk, her tiny frame as thin and as wiry as an adolescent's, seemed to expand to the size of a monster truck. She cracked her neck twice and took in a lungful of sweat-soaked air, just stopping short of beating her chest. The teacher was almost trembling with excitement. Alana could hardly blame her. Not so long ago, Alana had knocked the coach out in a bout of kickboxing. Kusmuk must be *dying* for an opportunity to pay her back.

"Note that you should always exploit the weaknesses of your opponent, and maximize your own strengths," she explained, sweeping Alana's legs from under her. "To do this, you have to keep your mind sharp and focused. Use your brain. Fight smart and then it doesn't matter if your opponent is faster. (*Ooof*). Stronger. (*Arrgh*). Better. (*Ullullull*)." Alana found herself looking at the ceiling once more. "You will always win." There was a humming in Alana's ears. Then she realized Coach Kusmuk was singing. If she strained her ears she could hear her. "... simply remember our favorite things are so bad..."

That's strange. It sounded very different when Miss Beatrice sang it.

Pffft. The air in Alana's lungs made a bid for escape. Alana wished she could do the same. But even though she was being pummeled and pulled, thrown and shoved, Alana felt a strange sense of gratitude to be there.

"Are you okay?" Sofia's worried face appeared next to hers. Alana swayed as she got up. There were four Sofias belly dancing in front of her eyes.

Sofia felt a tug on her arm. It was Maddie. "Don't worry about Alana," she said with a defiant glance at the smirking coach. "She's a lot tougher than she looks."

In the background of her vision Alana saw Khalilah fend off the attacks of her P.E. partner with ease. By using her weight to her advantage, she remained as unmoveable as a boulder. Flynn, as an Army brat, was as comfortable in hand-to-hand combat as he was on the dance floor, and sidestepped all the kicks and blows that came his way. Miller was not having an easy time but in an odd way seemed to enjoy being thrown about the room with Neanderthal abandon. With five older brothers, Alana didn't expect any less of her friend, Sofia.

"'Sbetter than ballroom dancing," she repeated to herself, although not sounding as convinced as before. Kusmuk used the momentum of one of Alana's wild punches to throw her effortlessly to the ground. Alana rolled onto her back with a groan. "I'm okay!" She held up a hand to tell the crowd of faces that came to check on her. She was eager to reassure them it wasn't anything serious. "'m okay. I don'need t'go to the..." The room swam again. "... clinic."

"Oh, but I think a visit to the clinic is EXACTLY what you need," said Coach Kusmuk.

Revenge. Kusmuk's eyes said. Her grim smile

was the last thing Alana saw before she blacked out, happier than Alana had ever seen her.

The coach had found her banana.

CHAPTER 35

A shocking discovery

Darling Lala, (Alana read)

Auntie Ling Ling and I are taking Auntie Katriona on a road trip to celebrate her 30th birthday. Late, I know, but it's the only thing which will get her out of bed and hopefully out of the doldrums. Unless we don't see Kylie Minogue, in which case … BUT we'll cross that bridge when we come to it. We will be back in plenty of time for the Big Game, so not long. Grandma dropped off some food – see the freezer – which should tide you over until I get back.

Guess what? I bumped into our lovely new neighbors, you know the ones who moved in across the road, and they have promised to keep an eye on you. So nice to have some friends move in (finally!) who are of a similar age.

Miss you already.

Forever. For always. No matter what.
Mamadoodlekins
xoxoxoxoxo

P.S. I've sorted out that problem you were telling
me about and the new neighbors are ecstatic to
help. I won't say anymore because I don't want
to spoil the surprise but I can't WAIT for your
birthday!

For once, Alana reflected, her mom's timing
was perfect. Alana could quite safely sneak out
of her house to snoop on the neighbors without
disturbing Emma, who preferred to work in the
downstairs study through the night. Alana did not
want to think about what role her new neighbors
were going to play in her birthday, but if it was
anything like past birthdays, it couldn't be good.
She pushed away the negative thoughts – it was a
couple of months before her birthday, after all –
and concentrated on the task at hand.

The night she chose was a cloudy one so that
the moon was a muted orb. It was eight days
since the note and seven days since a scratchy

phone call confirmed her mom was alive and well. ("Hello? *Crrsh. Hiss.* Alana? Can ... hear m-? *Crrsh. Beep, beep, beep.*) Alana had to wait until ten o'clock before Mr. Löfgren's car turned into their driveway. She slipped into a black tracksuit and exchanged her heavy boots for a pair of old trainers. Alana looked at the pink ski mask in her hand – something she'd found stashed in the back of a cupboard – and decided against it. It would be hard to use her "I'm-just-returning-your-mail" excuse with it on. Alana put the stash of letters she'd collected over the week into her backpack, and headed out into the cold.

A quick glance to her left revealed the silhouette of Mr. Peyton hunched over what was probably a crossword or Sudoku puzzle. It was a favorite pasttime of his and something he brought with him on the occasions he'd had to babysit Alana in the past. To the right was the familiar blue glow from Mrs. Whetu's TV and the sounds of *The Late, Late Show* on full volume. Good. Neither neighbor would catch her skulking around in the dead of night. But just to be sure, Alana avoided the streetlights and stuck to the shadows.

Although the walk to the neighbor's house was barely two minutes away, it felt like hours to Alana's pounding heart. The spooky house looked even more ominous in the dark and the climbing vines seemed to hold the house in a death grip. Alana skirted the neighbor's front yard and approached the house from behind, an area she had never been before. It was too late to hope the Löfgren's didn't have a guard dog. She could hardly scare a raging Alsatian with a bill for electricity.

The tepid light of a fluorescent bulb spilled from a window onto a ledge behind a row of wheelie bins lining the rear wall of the house. Alana decided this was as good a place to start as any, and tested the ledge for stability with the palms of her hands. A sudden bark from behind sent Alana scrambling prematurely, staring fearfully into the dark. *Panting. Sounds ragged. Very close by*, she panted raggedly, until she realized the breathing was her own. She touched her ribs gingerly which were still tender from Kusmuk's P.E. session. She was lucky her friends had been there to fend Nurse Cathy off. Otherwise the nurse may not have stopped at bandaging only her side. When she'd calmed down, she realized the dog was behind the neighbor's fence on the street behind. Not their dog. Not a threat. At least, not within biting distance.

Alana shivered, and not just from the wintry temperatures. She turned to face the window which was covered in vines. Alana pulled some of it away gently. She used the edge of her sleeve to scrub away the grime on the glass. At first glance the room looked empty, until Alana looked, really looked, and realized this was not the case. The walls displayed masks of all types and sizes – African, Asian, Pacific Islander - with large gaping holes for eyes and mouths, and hair fashioned from a variety of animals and grasses. If this wasn't disturbing enough, the rest of the room stood in stark contrast, from the hospital tiles on the floor to the shelves of scientific equipment. But what was really alarming was Mr. Löfgren bent over a body which was lying on a trolley with wheels.

The hunched figure in black straightened suddenly, or as much as his bent back allowed. He turned to face the windows. Alana held her breath as his hooked nose twitched and thin lips parted to reveal a line of pointy teeth. She leaned back into the shadows, holding some of the vine in front of her face for cover. He took a few steps toward her. The vine shook. If he came any closer he was sure to spot her. His head whipped around at the jarring sound of the telephone. With one final indecisive look in Alana's direction, he left the room with hurried footsteps. The vine dropped. Alana leaned her forehead against the cool pane of glass before taking a shaky breath.

That was close.

What was that mysterious body and was it still alive? With Mr. Löfgren's strange hobby of stuffing and recombining animals, was it even real? With no thought other than the driving need to know, Alana tested the windows for a way in. There wasn't much time. The edge of one window was slightly ajar but stiff from a lack of use. For anyone but Alana, this would have been a problem, but a quick search of her backpack yielded a spray can of oil which loosened the hinges. It was the same spray she'd used to make a "quiet" entrance into food technology class last year with celebrity chef Isabella Thornton. Thanks to Flynn, it hadn't worked. *Flynn*. Alana squashed the impulse to make a soppy sigh and opened the window large enough to slide through.

Thud!!!

Not Alana's most graceful entrance, but it didn't bring anyone running. She approached the body on tiptoe, one trainer at a time. It brought her to where the body lay, much faster than she liked.

The woman was dead still. The woman was dead quiet. Let's face it. The woman was DEAD. She was grandma-old and dressed in what was probably her best outfit – for isn't that how we dress the dead? In formal clothes they were rarely comfortable in? The skin on her face was paper thin. Alana could see veins. Capillaries. A wrinkled neck. But it was not these details which captured her attention. It was the woman's hair. So white it was almost transparent, and pulled back into ... Alana took a moment to check ... yep, a bun.

Have you ever seen fireworks? That's how the epiphany felt when it hit Alana. Like a series of blinding flashes of colored light going off in her brain. *Boom! Crash! Kapow!*

Will's dad, Vlad, comes from Sweden and mine are from Ireland, so we suffer terribly from sunburn and avoid the outdoors wherever possible. I'm sure that's why we've all got such terrible circulation, and of course Alice's skin is so delicate. Phooey! *Steak tartare tastes wonderful! We often eat food raw. So many nutrients are lost after cooking.* Baloney! *Have the children still got that silly game? Will's always messing around. I'm sorry if he scared you.* Yeah, right!

But then, Emma's note...

P.S. I've sorted out that problem you were

telling me about and the new neighbors are ecstatic to help.

If Alana squinted, replaced the outfit with sequins or frills, and placed a feathery, fruity headdress on the dead woman's head...

C.R.U.D!

No wonder Ballroom Dancing classes had been "canceled until further notice." Their ballroom dancing teacher was lying dead in the Löfgren's basement!

CHAPTER 36

A detour through Woop-Woop

While Alana was maneuvering Mrs. Cronenberg's dead body out of the Löfgren's window, Katriona, Ling Ling, and Emma were in the throes of their own struggle in Australia's Outback. The python with the strange lump inside its body had moved on. The bird of prey resumed its original position to bide its time, and beyond the bird, through the bush scrub, and up the hill, Emma and her friends were being watched.

The three women remained unaware.

Instead, they focused their efforts on contacting civilization with no success. The phone was out of range and losing power. ("Hello? *Crrsh. Hiss.* Alana? Can you hear me? *Crrsh. Beep, beep, beep.*) An attempt to send smoke signals started a small bushfire. In preparation for an aerial search, they found only enough rocks to spell "S.O." Therefore when Emma's mobile phone rang – one bar of battery remaining – the three women stared at it in amazement.

"Tell them I need sunscreen!"

"Tell them I need my loofah!

"Find out who won *Star Search*!"

"Did Jane end up marrying Kurt?"

"I think we need gas. Send gas!"

"And ice!"

"And those cute little umbrellas for drinks!"

But the futility of making any request became obvious as soon as they realized it must be a Friday, and therefore who had called...

"Oh," said Emma. "Hi, Mom."

The three women were unlikely to get their sunscreen, loofah, or gas, much less be rescued any time soon because Emma – as usual – could hardly get a word in edgeways.

"That's great news, Mom, but I need you to... Hello? Mom? Are you still there?" Emma banged the phone on the nearest hard surface she could find to reconnect.

"Ow," cried Ling Ling, rubbing her forehead.

Emma threw the phone away in frustration. Trust her luck. The only call with clear reception and all Emma had was an invitation to another wedding. And now the battery was dead. Just like they were going to be if they didn't get out of here. Unless they could find clean drinking water. Fast. But nobody relished the idea of getting lost in the desert, with red earth stretching as far as their sunglasses could see. After several hours, desperation drove them to explore and after much cajoling, Ling Ling was persuaded to empty the contents of her designer luggage to create a trail. It was a curious and somewhat startling sight for the wildlife that stumbled upon her *Miu Miu* mules and *Paul Frank* pajamas. But at least, Katriona assured them, the trail wouldn't get eaten up, unlike what happened to Hansel and Gretel, which just goes to show you how stupid children could be.

Ling Ling, her water "divining rod," dipping and swerving in dehydration-fueled fury, shot Katriona a look filled with loathing. Stupid children? What about stupid friends? It wasn't *Katriona's* stupid luggage being scattered all over the place. In fact, if it wasn't for Katriona and her stupid stubbornness, they wouldn't even be here and they'd still own The Beauty Bar today, Ling Ling told her.

"WHAT?!"

Even Emma, who was lost in the fantasy of flinging confetti down an aisle, paused to stare.

"What could I do, Katriona?" Ling Ling raged. "How was I supposed to do all the nails, hair, makeup, and restyling with you in bed? Thirty? Big deal! Just say you're 20-*plus* and you can stay in your twenties forever! Stoo-pid kuku-bird! Orbi quek if we pok kai orready!" Ling Ling yelled, reverting to Singlish in her frustration. Stupid idiot! Serves you right if we're already bankrupt!

Katriona charged and ran at Ling Ling. Her long fingers found Ling Ling's throat and drove the slim woman backward. Back, back, back... all the way into a pool of water. Katriona and Ling Ling were knee-deep in blessed coolness before they realized where they were. The water made them forget their quarrel. Emma dive-bombed after them. They scrubbed their faces. They rinsed their hair. They watched as the red earth that caked their skin and clothes turned muddy and floated away in a thick film.

The three women were not the only ones enjoying the water. A flock of white birds with thin sticks for legs dipped their heads into the water for food. A pair of kangaroos bent down once, twice, three times, before bounding off on huge powerful legs. Knobbly, brown logs bobbed gently on the water's surface. With eyes closed the air smelled sweeter, greener. All was still until Emma broke the silence.

"But what about this 'Fok Wee Mung' woman? She sounds like the kind of person who might hurt you."

"If she *just* hurts me," Ling Ling said. "I'll be very lucky."

Katriona let out a grunt of protest because even though Ling Ling had landed them in the middle of nowhere, killed her pet cat, Jinx, and lost their business to gambling, Ling Ling was still her best friend.

"No, no, no," Ling Ling corrected, "It's Fok *Wee*."

...

Emma was the first to emerge from the water. She gathered up her unruly hair and squeezed. The water dripped and formed a puddle before disappearing into the parched earth. Nearby, an old sign lay on the ground where it had fallen. The posts were rotted and some of the lettering was missing. She read it quietly to herself.

Beware of crocodiles.

Swim at your own risk.

Welcome to Mugga Mugga Resort! Only now it read: *...come to Mug.. ....a ..sort!*

Ling Ling's tremulous voice caught Emma's attention. "Ummm, Katriona, maybe you should stop riding that brown log."

CHAPTER 37

Fact 5. Pickles make you fart

Fact 1: Wheelbarrows were very handy.

Fact 2: The Big Game was tomorrow.

Fact 3: Sometimes four heads were NOT better than one.

Fact 4: There was someone at the door.

Alana found list-writing strangely comforting but none of the facts she'd written were of any help. Although Sofia, Khalilah, and Maddie reduced their panicked cries of "*CrudCrudCrud,*" "*Omigodomigodomigod,*" and "*Wearesodeadsodeadsodead*" to a whisper, it still wasn't helping! And when the knocking at the door continued, they could barely contain their alarm.

A rattle at the front door fused their feet to the ground. Whoever it was had a key! A part of Alana relaxed. Rule out her mother. But if it wasn't her mom, then it must be –

"Lola!"

"Alana!"

Alana was enveloped in a huge hug and her cheeks were pinched. Then Mrs. Corazon reproached Alana for not eating enough, before being introduced to each of her granddaughter's friends. Although she barely came up to Alana's shoulder, Mrs. Corazon had a big personality which gave the impression she was much taller. Her hair was short and tightly permed, framing a face that was heart-shaped and lightly wrinkled. She favored big jewelry and a lifetime of long dangly earrings had stretched her lobes into the shape of a teardrop. Clusters of rings covered her fingers and thick bangles jangled on her wrists. While her mom always smelled of sun-kissed peaches, Alana's grandmother used a perfume that smelled of baby cologne, which she claimed was the secret to keeping her young. Mrs. Corazon placed her hands on her ample hips and looked around.

"There's something different," she said, tapping her pursed lips. The four girls looked worried.

"Has your mom been doing D.I.Y. again?" Two sharp brown eyes scanned the room.

At this, each of the girls scrambled into different poses to shield the dead body from Mrs. Corazon's gaze. Khalilah planted her feet and stretched her arms theatrically with a yawn. Maddie shuffled like a bobbing crab. Sofia flicked her hair and Alana grabbed her grandmother's hand whenever she strayed toward the coffee table, to steer her away. "It's so nice to see you, Lola."

"It's nice to see you too, Alana," Mrs. Corazon said warmly, before marching the room's perimeter. "I know! You got a new couch!" But before Alana could answer, she disagreed with herself. "No, no, that's not it. New picture? No. Painting? No. Curtains? No." Thirty minutes and two cups of tea later, Mrs. Corazon was still stumped.

It didn't look like anything was going to make Mrs. Corazon leave until the dead body let out a stream of gas so loud and long, there was no mistaking what the sound was.

"It wasn't *me*!" cried Khalilah indignantly, mid-stretch.

"Okay," grumbled Maddie through clenched teeth, "I guess it was me, then," with a meaningful look at Khalilah who was in front of the body and therefore the more likely candidate.

"Don't worry, dear. It always happens to me with pickles. I love them but they do hideous things to the body," she confided to Maddie graciously, patting her rounded stomach. She squinted at her watch, too vain to wear glasses. "Is that the time? I'd better get going. It's a long way back to Campbelltown. But," she hesitated, "I really don't like leaving you on your own like this. Are you sure you're going to be alright?"

Alana was quick to reassure her. "I'll be fine. Truly. The girls are staying over to study. Plus there's all that food you left me in the freezer."

"Well, alright then. If you're *really* sure." Alana's grandmother was glad she'd made enough food to feed an army. She pitched forward to put her cup on the coffee table where the dead body lay. The girls threw themselves upon her, wrestling it from her clasp. "Such good girls. So well brought up and helpful," she cooed.

Alana's grandmother heaved herself from the couch and gave her granddaughter one last hug. "Your mom said she'd be home soon when I talked to her on Friday, so it won't be long. Goodbye, darling," she said. "Remember. Eat more."

"I will, Lola. Thanks, Lola. Bye, Lola," Alana said, resisting the urge to drag her outside.

"And don't worry," Mrs. Corazon said with a wagging finger as she said goodbye, "it will come to me. I'll figure out what's different. Bye-bye now. Study hard! Good luck for tomorrow's game!"

With Mrs. Corazon finally out the door they found Khalilah staring at the dead body with a grin. "She must have had a *lot* of pickles," she decided.

...

It was late afternoon when there was another knock on the Oakley door.

"Hooroo! I've got your mail!"

A beady eye like a blue marble peered through the window, but the curtains were drawn. Mrs. Whetu made a sound of annoyance and eyed the wheelbarrow by the door. She stashed the mail – one insurance letter and three flyers advertising new restaurants – back in her purse. She would try again later. In the meantime she had to conjure a story about the Oakleys and their strange friends. The gels at the RSL were restless. The suspicious-looking wheelbarrow and emphatically closed curtains made a good start...

CHAPTER 38

Dead to the world

The next thing you'll notice about the body is that it has a new headdress made from fruit, tinsel, and three mini disco balls. A feather boa is wrapped around its neck. The girls seem pleased with their efforts. It seems right somehow. "Stop looking at me," Khalilah tells the corpse before flipping it over. She joins her three friends upstairs. They are in Alana's bedroom. At Alana's insistence, the music is loud. It is easier for her to think when the drums, guitar, and bass make the walls shake. And with Alana's head crammed with sound, it is difficult for images of the corpse to sneak into her brain. Alana's theory that the Löfgren's are vampires sounds ridiculous at first, but the dead body in the living room punctuates everyone's denial with a question mark. Although nobody wants to lose the body, nobody wants to sleep with it either, so they retreat upstairs. They take turns to keep a lookout – fearful of the slightest sound on the stairs.

Alana's bedroom, like Sofia's, reflects her personality. While Sofia's room is like a gypsy caravan hinting at hidden treasures, Alana's is zen-like and unapologetic. A bookshelf fashioned from an old skateboard carries a set of Shakespeare's graphic novels – last year's birthday present from her three friends. Important dates are circled on her calendar. Crimson curtains and turquoise walls provide the perfect backdrop for her pet rock, Rocky, and a framed photograph of Alana and her dad, with matching dimples, clutching guitars. The much bigger guitar that Alana uses now stands in the corner of the room. The full-length silhouette cutout of Jimi Hendrix on the wall assumes a new menacing shape.

What do we do now? Four pairs of eyes say to each other. Eventually they decide on a horror movie and grab each other, screaming, during the scary bits.

Nobody goes downstairs for popcorn.

This explains why the four girls didn't hear Mrs. Whetu knocking, or later on, the arrival of Boris the Imbécile. Boris looks at the instructions in his hand: *Pick up blue bird. Deliver to The Bar.* The instructions are from James O'Keefe. A photographer. Some guy the Lucianos hooked him up with, who needs the occasional gofer. This suits Boris who uses his spare time to earn extra cash. There is a postscript. *If no one is home, use the key under the garden gnome.* Boris lifts the sculpture – a squat figurine with a manic grin holding a fishing rod – and finds the key. It slides in easily. He opens the door and it swings open into a darkened hall. Dramatic music from a horror film blares upstairs. There are high-pitched squeals and nervous laughter. Boris hurries in and leaves the door ajar. Now that he knows someone is home he wants to get on with the job without interference. "Blue bird, blue bird," he mutters. The room on the left has a large Christmas tree, desk, and daybed. No birds in there. The room on the right is the living room. He spots a purple flamingo in the corner. It is standing on one leg. He moves toward it, but then spots an old bird on the coffee table, face down. Boris is good at thinking on his feet.

Only one of them is *blue*.

Boris is the second person to be grateful for the wheelbarrow in the front yard and Mrs. Whetu – staring until she loses sight of Boris, the dead body, and the wheelbarrow – adds more juicy details to her story for the RSL.

CHAPTER 39

Outback adventures

Mugga Mugga Resort, or "Mug.. ....a ..sort," according to the decrepit sign, originally opened in the hope of attracting high-end tourists with lots of cash and limited time. It failed. It turned out that quaint outdoor toilets and koala-embroidered towels did not appeal to those kinds of tourists. It did attract wildlife scientists, though, or one wildlife scientist in particular, who was seeking the elusive "Luna Lumen Succo" or Moonglow Spider, said to hatch during the winter solstice. Dr. Molloy had spent the last thirty years booked in a room at the Mugga Mugga Resort to track it down. To his scientific peers, Dr. Molloy was a crackpot chasing the arachnid equivalent of the Bunyip. They insisted the Moonglow Spider and its link to pagans, druids, ley lines, and stone circles didn't exist. Their derision only made Molloy more determined.

It didn't help that the Moonglow Spider was said to suck blood from its victims. It was normally the size of a thumbnail with thin fangs that extended when it opened its jaw. Unlike the Red Back Spider with its distinctive red markings, or the Funnel Web Spider with its long spinnerets, the Moonglow Spider looked like an ordinary-looking creepy-crawly until viewed in the dark. In the dark, it glowed as white and as bright as the moon of its namesake so that it looked like a fallen star. But the arachnid could switch the light on and off like a firefly, which made it almost impossible to identify. The only time it couldn't was during the annual hatching period. At this time, it grew to the size of a child's palm from tip to toe, with a light as bright as a beacon until all the eggs hatched. Dr. Molloy suspected it was so that the spiderlings had a guiding light but this was just a theory as he had never witnessed it. It was also said to be the safest time to observe the spider because it went into a trance, like turtles did when they laid their eggs on the beach.

For the last thirty years, Dr. Molloy had been in the wrong place at the right time and had no luck collecting the evidence to prove any of his theories. But he had a strong feeling this year would be different. Dr. Molloy tracked the spider's trail to a remote part of the resort where a strange group of women had set up camp. Even to Dr. Molloy's untrained eye they looked a sorry sight. The women had gone swimming in the billabong pool and were sitting in a bedraggled heap around a small fire. They appeared to be on an odd diet of biscuits and sweets. Their clothes lay in a messy, dirty pile next to the massive, philosophical "SO" they had spelled out with rocks. So ... *here we are?* So ... *beautiful?* So ... *what?*

Molloy didn't understand. Dr. Molloy never "roughed it" himself unless it was in the name of science. One year he sat and waited for the hatching of the Moonglow Spider in the "shelter" of a giant cactus from dusk to dawn, only to find it was the wrong spider. Most other days, though, Molloy availed himself of the resort's facilities.

They served three decent meals a day – sausages and baked beans for breakfast, lunch, and dinner – the jacuzzi was pleasant, and the swimming pool was clean, refreshing, and crocodile-free. On top of all that, Mugga Mugga was over the hill, less than fifty meters away. He wondered why they even bothered to camp. *Tourists*, he allowed himself a condescending chuckle, *bless 'em*.

It was unfortunate for the arachnid specialist that these particular tourists had chosen the Moonglow Spider's hatch site, or more specifically, had chosen to park their camper van on top of it. But no matter, decided the indomitable scientist, he would overcome this barrier too. In fact, he wondered whether the encasing darkness of the camper van might even work in his favor and belie a telltale glow at the time of hatching. The scientist looked up at the moon which hung low in the sky and mentally prepared his scrawny behind for a long, numbing wait.

The three women sat in silence around the campfire thirty meters downhill from where

Molloy was seated on a flat rock. The packet of biscuits was quickly exhausted and they moved on to marshmallows which they stabbed with sticks and held over the flames. Emma rubbed futilely at her hair to help it dry. Katriona and Ling Ling chewed on the melted goo, in between exchanging glances when they thought the other wasn't looking. Neither of them wanted to be the first to speak.

Emma decided to check the van to escape the uncomfortable silence. The hood yielded no further secrets and the underside of the car remained just as inscrutable. Nothing was on fire, the alternator was working, and all wires seemed intact. It looked like a bit of gas was all they needed to be back on their way.

"Well, goodnight, then," Emma said, emerging from underneath the car, brushing off the dust and opening the rear door of the van where she was aching to crash. It had been another long, hot, tiring day.

Katriona and Ling Ling looked up to say

goodnight and at the same time noticed the dark shadow on the back of Emma's T-shirt. The spider took on almost alien properties as it began to swell and then glow. Ling Ling responded with lightning reflexes. She leapt up and pounded Emma's back with her marshmallow stick. Katriona joined in with hers. Then to both their horror, tiny, flashing bulbs exploded from the spider's sac. Only Dr. Molloy knew what they were – spiderlings spinning draglines and ballooning away. After thirty years of ridicule, here was the evidence! Finally! He pounded down the hill as fast as his thin legs could carry him. The nightscope swung wildly around his neck. But there was no escaping Ling Ling and Katriona. They were determined to kill first and ask questions later. They whacked at the sparks until each one winked out of existence. They dragged the T-shirt from Emma's body to stomp on it. They crumpled the T-shirt into a ball of insect bits and goo and flung it on the fire. It shot flames a meter high with a bone-sucking *whoomph*.

From a distance came a plaintive cry, "Noooooooooooooooooooooo!"

...

Mugga Mugga Resort had everything the three women desired: hot water, a TV, and even the little colorful umbrellas for drinks! Thirty minutes later, Katriona and Ling Ling were laughing like old times and Emma was relishing the luxury of blow-drying her hair dry. Katriona, in particular, was in high spirits, especially now Ling Ling had shown her how – with a bit of mathematical hocus pocus – she could remain in her 20s forever. Now all they needed was to figure out how to get rid of this Fok Wee Mung character, and get The Beauty Bar back. But all thoughts of figuring out that problem flew out the window the minute Katriona spotted the evening news.

"Arnie!" Katriona cried, pointing at the screen.

There was a streaker. It was Arnie! Headless

Arnie from next door was running naked across a soccer field. Although the streaker wore a mask, Katriona and Ling Ling knew it was him. They were sure of it. As the camera zoomed in on the streaker's twin cheeks which read "Free Tibet!" they were convinced.

Ling Ling looked at it thoughtfully. "So *that's* what that tattoo is! Pity we still can't see his face."

Eyebrow arched high as she contemplated the naked, physical accomplishment of a daily workout, Katriona replied, "Who cares about his *face*?"

The significance of the soccer match had a different meaning for Emma. The hairdryer dropped with a *clang* from her hand. If today was Saturday, then tomorrow was... "Oh no! Alana's Big Game!"

...

In the dead of night, four young university students checked in to the Mugga Mugga Resort after parking their Kombi van next to another. The four took great pleasure comparing the two cars – alternately slapping each other and collapsing incoherently as they pointed from one to the other: "Mermaid. Hahaha. Mango. Hahaha. Mermaid. Hahaha."

...

In the dead of night, exactly five minutes later, three women checked *out* of the Mugga Mugga Resort. On their way to the car park, they passed a man huddled by the pool. It was the man who had rescued them from the desert. He was a forlorn figure as he cradled a brightly colored cocktail in shaking hands. He was moaning. "Thirty years! Thirty *stupid* years!" the man repeated, as he rocked back and forth in a stupor.

"Uh uh uh," a wagging fingernail of polished leopard spots told him. "Just say you're twenty-*plus* and you can stay in your twenties forever!" With that Good Deed done and ten minutes of jiggling, they managed to unlock the van and begin driving back to Newtown.

If they were lucky, they might just make it to The Big Game.

CHAPTER 40

Horror of horrors

Alana first found out about her mom's impending arrival via the morning news. She felt such a strange sense of déjà vu she had to sit down on the couch. Everybody else was upstairs getting ready. It had been a sleepless night for the four of them. The horror movie had been a bad idea. It's hard to sleep with one eye open. Alana shook her head at the TV like a cow faced with trigonometry. According to the news report, three women had hijacked a giant mango and were being pursued by police. Then the camera showed Auntie Katriona with a flowing sari. On the roof of a Kombi van. (Not theirs, Alana noted). Clinging to a three-meter mango. Ling Ling was in the driver's seat. And her mom was jumping up and down in the front seat while a police car followed closely behind.

Chapter 40

By the time the Madzaini household switched on their TV, two police cars were part of the high-speed car chase. Jefri, holding the cover of a *Priscilla: Queen of the Desert*-DVD, cried, "Those movies *are* real. I knew she was lying!"

When the Luciano's switched on theirs, there were three police cars.

"Another funny dream," chuckled the bedridden Luca.

The Dawson family were in time to see a second news helicopter join the hunt.

When four university students at the Mugga Mugga Resort looked up from their breakfast, they saw *their* Kombi van, with *their* stolen three-meter mango blazing a trail across the desert. They could not hear Ling Ling ask Katriona if she'd found the GPS in her bag on the roof. They could not hear Katriona yelling directions, nor could they hear Emma's response. All they could hear was the reporter. One of the university students began crushing the box of cereal until there was nothing but crumbs left inside. His dream of pulling off the most daring prank in the history of the university was fading with every kilometer.

In a small office above a bakery in the heart of Sydney's Chinatown, pumpkin seeds were being crushed by the best porcelain chompers money could buy. The discs of an abacus flicked up and down. Two eyes stared in different directions. One eye was fixed on the numbers in a tiny black book. The other was trained on the unfolding drama on TV.

A voice barked to a waiting lackey: "Shu Ling Ling. It is time to collect."

Tick tock tick tock. Ling Ling was out of time.

CHAPTER 41

Dead and gone

Khalilah, Maddie, and Sofia joined Alana on the couch to watch Emma and her friends on TV. Sofia passed Alana a slice of toast, which she chewed on without thinking. Alana sighed with a look at the clock. They were running late. There was probably a logical explanation why her mom was in a stolen vehicle with a giant mango on the roof of the car. There always was. But she didn't have time to find out. She had a dead body to deal with and a soccer game to play.

Alana asked Sofia to pass the remote so she could switch off the television, before putting her plate on the coffee table. The *clink* of ceramic made her frown. Her gaze dropped. *The coffee table.*

"Where is the body?" Alana's voice was barely a whisper.

Sofia was on her hands and knees looking for the remote control. "What do you want, the remote or the body?"

"The body!" Alana cried.

"The body!" Khalilah repeated.

"Where's the body?" Maddie yelled.

The question echoed off the curtains. The search became frenzied. They discovered magazines, a mug that read "Instant human: Just add coffee," and a Pink Floyd CD. They found the remote control. What they *didn't* find was the body. And as they searched, nobody voiced the question on everybody's lips. Was the dead body now ... *a vampire?* A loud rap on the door made them squeal. All eyes turned to Alana who dived for the curtains and hissed over her shoulder. "It's Uncle James. He's here to take us to the game."

Alana switched off the television and smoothed down her hair before opening the front door. "Hi, Uncle James. Sorry, I'm not ready yet. Won't be long. Grab a coffee, if you like," she gabbled.

The first thing James noticed when he entered the living room was the flamingo statue. Damn! It was still here and he'd specifically asked Boris to deliver it to the Brothers' Bar for a photoshoot of the new restaurant. He supposed that's what you got for employing someone with the words "The Imbécile" embroidered on the back of their leather jacket. He shrugged his broad shoulders and swept back his hair with impatient fingers. It had grown long again.

The next thing James noticed was the girls' white faces. They looked terrified. By the state of the living room he guessed they had been practicing soccer moves. After all, this was it. The Big Game! The game against the Soccer Academy's Bluejay Barbarians! No wonder they were nervous. The competitor within him kicked into high gear and he began a rousing pep talk, fist slamming into palm.

"You can do this. Just give it everything you've got. Remember to work as a team. Everyone attacks. Everyone defends."

The three friends tidied up the living room. They rearranged the furniture and cleared the floor – still hopeful the body was under a cushion – with half an ear on James' speech. Their preoccupation did not go unnoticed.

"Come on," James roared. "Let me hear you say, Go Gibbons!"

"Go Gibbons!" they repeated mechanically.

"You can do better than that. Go Gibbons!"

They tried again. "Go Gibbons!" And at James' insistence, continued to chant "Go Gibbons!" all the way to his car. Mrs. Whetu's beady eyes stayed trained on them through her window, mentally making notes.

Alana heaved the kit bags into the Mini Cooper's trunk and slammed it shut with a last glance at her home, and then the spooky house across the road. The question remained unanswered.

Where was the body now?

...

Do you want to know where the body is? I'll give you three guesses. It's not at the Brothers' Bar in Surry Hills. It's not even at the local pub on King Street. Where did Boris the Imbécile make his delivery?

Emma, Katriona, and Ling Ling were about to find out...

CHAPTER 42

Lift-off

The Sunday news presenter was having a field day. High-speed car chases were a dime a dozen but one rarely reported one with such dramatic footage. The original feature about Sookie the Surfing Dog got shoved aside for the news that there was a giant mango on the run, with a Priscilla-look-a-like dumping the contents of a suitcase at pursuing police. Katriona was not doing it on purpose. As soon as she unzipped the designer luggage, Ling Ling's sari whipped out and wrapped itself around Katriona's eyes. She managed to bring it down to her neck so she could rummage through the rest of the bag for the GPS but things kept flying out. Katriona stopped to look around and realized that if she peered *around* the giant mango, she could see where exactly they should be going. Maybe they didn't need the GPS after all? With full confidence, she yelled, "Straight ahead," to Ling Ling, and "Overtake, or get lost," to the four police cars behind her. The sirens were driving her mad.

Ling Ling was in complete agreement with Katriona. She gestured to the police cars to drive past her and when they didn't, she sped up to avoid them. It was very stressful. It didn't help that Emma was sitting next to her, bouncing up and down. "The time! Look at the time!" And then Ling Ling saw him – one of the many strangers whom Ling Ling recognized as part of the odd collection of people she waved to from her apartment every morning – a truck driver parked on the other side of the road. A truck driver, she realized, who could give them directions...

"Hold on," she yelled up at Katriona, who grabbed the bag straps just in time.

Ling Ling executed a perfect U-turn and slammed on the brakes so that she was eye-to-eye with the semitrailer. The driver, a whiskered fellow with rheumy blue eyes, a bulbous red nose, and a gold tooth, recognized her as the-woman-in-the-window whom he had never met, but who he waved to on King Street as he passed through the big city. He took another slurp of coffee from his flask. Ling Ling stepped out of the van.

It looked like that was about to change.

The four police cars did not predict Ling Ling's intention and therefore ended up in each other's laps with a squeal of brakes and bone-crunching metal, eighty meters away. Their abrupt course created deep furrows in the red earth next to the highway and several dings in the chassis. As Ling Ling explained their predicament to the truck driver – which way to Newtown? – a second helicopter from a rival channel landed and a reporter emerged.

Back in the television studio, the news presenter wished she could lip-read because her producer was screaming in her earpiece to find out what was going on. By the look of it, the truck driver, the three women and the two news reporters were in negotiations, while the four-car pile-up of police cars formed a messy stack in the background. She was live-to-air and everything had to be done with a smile.

She smiled.

"Stay tuned to Sunday Morning Express. We'll have more exciting action for you, after the break."

...

"The time! The time!" Emma reminded them all.

"They could take you," the truck driver said, gesturing with his head at the helicopters.

"Absolutely!" the two reporters said together and then frowned. A bidding war ensued. Both wanted to question this intriguing trio of women about their oversized cargo.

The three women shrugged. It wasn't as if the police were in a position to help, staggering about their battered cars in bewilderment, so they said goodbye to the truck driver, retrieved their luggage, and became airborne with the helicopter with the most room for their belongings.

"Firstly, anything you'd like to say to our audience out there?" the successful reporter asked the three women with a smug wave at his rival.

Ling Ling looked down. The camera followed her gaze and honed in on the crash site before lifting. "Don't speed," she said solemnly to the lens.

CHAPTER 43

The battle begins

Coach McNeeson was worried. Apart from Prita and Preyasi, the rest of the Gibson Gibbons were unusually sluggish and bleary-eyed. Admittedly it was 9 o'clock on a freezing Sunday morning, and the frost on the grass had barely begun to melt, but McNeeson had hoped they'd be psyched with the home team advantage. Even though all their supporters were in Gibbons colors chanting encouragement, however, it failed to register with the girls.

"Buck up," the gentle Scotsman chided, "I've seen zombies more alive than you." At this, Sofia shrieked and took off for the girl's toilets. Coach McNecson looked startled, his bushy eyebrows rising like two furry half-moons.

Alana excused the team and went into a private huddle. "We have to pull ourselves together," she urged everybody. "If we don't," she said with a worried look at the Barbarians doing one-armed push-ups, "we are SO dead."

With this sobering thought in mind, they returned to McNeeson's warm-up and refocused. It wasn't easy but they stopped checking over their shoulder for a walking corpse. Coach McNeeson clapped his hands and gestured for a last minute talk. He reminded them that although the Barbarians looked stronger, faster, and more self-assured than their own team, the Barbarians didn't have what it took to win. Alana and her friends were mystified. The coach had just provided three solid reasons why the Gibbons were going to get beaten. What hope did they have?

"You," McNeeson said, his Adam's apple bobbing as he spoke with emotion, "know what it's like to lose and how to fight *on*!" He waved a hand at the opposition. "They haven't got a clue. They've never lost in their lives! That makes them vulnerable. Their arrogance is their downfall. Their overconfidence is their weak spot. Their pride makes them blind. I want you to keep at them like a dog with a bone." McNeeson bared his yellowing teeth. "I want you to be the stubborn camel that refuses to budge." He paced back and forth. "I want you to be the annoying mosquito that won't go away."

The girls looked thoughtful. They could be determined, stubborn, annoying. Hadn't all of them persevered in one way or another this year to achieve amazing things in the restaurant, on the violin, in the classroom, or on the skateboard? They might not be as physically strong as the Bluejay Barbarians, but the Gibbons could have the stronger *mind.*

"Uh-oh," Alana whispered.

"What?" asked Maddie, concerned.

"I think I just learned something profound from Coach Kusmuk!"

Thunderous shudders announced the arrival of a helicopter. Three gorilla mascots made their way down a rope ladder. They stopped halfway down and beat their chests. "Go Gorillas!"

(It looked like the stolen Kombi van had yielded

more than just a giant mango.)

"It's gibbons, not gorillas. Go *Gibbons!*" someone in the crowd yelled.

"Gorillas, gibbons, same-same lah!" one of the mascots said with a dismissive wave of a massive paw. The three of them descended to the field and lumbered toward Alana and her team.

"Hahaha," a snide voice chuckled, "still monkeying around, I see." It was Battle-Axe. The Bluejay Barbarian's coach. With the three gorilla mascots approaching from one end, and Sofia drawing a third eye on everyone's foreheads to ward off evil at the other, Coach McNeeson could see why Battle-Axe found the Gibbons amusing, laughable even. Heck, even he had to admit that behind all his brave talk, he was worried for his team. But the big difference between the Barbarians and the Gibbons – apart from ten centimeters and two kilos in weight – was that the Barbarians were individuals playing for personal glory, not a squad playing for the team. The Gibbons loved soccer and cared for each other. What they didn't have in muscle they made up for in team spirit. They had teamwork, and Coach McNeeson knew that together, they could pull off a win.

The little man aimed a vicious finger at McNeeson's chest. It was a stretch at 135 centimeters high so he was only able to bury his tiny digit into McNeeson's belly button. "I take this game seriously. You and your little band of misfits are nothing but a bad joke waiting to implode."

"We'll let our *feet* do the talking," McNeeson replied, stepping back from the belly button poke and warding off the wave of protests on his team's lips.

The referee's whistle blew.

The Bluejay Barbarians stopped arm-wrestling on the grass. Sofia finished "cleansing" the pitch with burning sage.

The battle began.

CHAPTER 44

Football frenzy

The Gibbons were struggling against the Bluejay Barbarians within the first ten minutes of the game. The Barbarians *were* stronger and faster, and it was all the Gibbons could do to steer clear of the beefy elbows that found their faces. In the eleventh minute, a kick from the Barbarians' Number 10 from the halfway line sent the ball soaring unexpectedly into the net.

Khalilah buried her face in her hands. "I'm sorry!" she cried, as Player Number 10 pumped her fist in the air and collected applause from the crowd.

"No worries, Khalilah!" the Gibbons reassured her. Alana had been expecting it. The Barbarians' Number 10 was a killer player with wicked footwork who was acutely possessive of the ball. Nobody else had touched it since the starting whistle, preferring to take a punt from the halfway line than pass. *And why not*, Alana shrugged. *It paid off, didn't it?* That was until the Barbarians' Number 10 tackled her own player to steal the ball soon after play resumed. A ripple of surprise ran through Alana's team. How big was this girl's ego? It was then that Alana realized the Barbarians' weakness. Number 10 never passed the ball. She was too intent on performing tricks, playing for herself, or claiming credit to work with her team, and she could tell it infuriated the other girls. The Gibbons may not be able to outrun the Barbarians or muscle their way out, but at least they had teamwork. Alana suggested a new strategy and the Gibbons felt the results within moments.

"I was open. I was right there," a Barbarian player berated their Number 10. "Why didn't you pass?" The Gibbons exchanged a triumphant look. They had converged on the one player without bothering to mark any of the others. The attempted kick for goal had been headed out of the way by Maddie, who gave everybody the thumbs-up sign before rubbing her head with a grin.

The next time the Barbarians' Number 10 had the ball and got blocked she *did* pass. But Alana was prepared for that too and intercepted it, pulling away with the ball down the field. Number 10 tore after her with a grunt of surprise and caught up, but Maddie had already collected the ball and was passing it to Prita. The ball disappeared down the field and was heading for the Gibbon's goal with a kick from Preyasi's boot. The Barbarians' goalkeeper rushed forward to grab the ball, just as another teammate ran up to boot it out of the way. There was a desperate fumble. Prita caught up and joined in, but by then the ball had rolled free of the three of them. Alana swerved and scooped it up with her boot, taking off for the *undefended* goal posts. The goalkeeper scrambled after her. It became a race. A race Alana wasn't sure she could win, so she flicked the ball to Maddie, just as player Number 10 descended on her, teeth bared. It was too little too late. Maddie took the shot and buried the ball deep into the net unimpeded.

Number 10 rounded on her teammates with a snarl. "See what happens when I pass the ball?"

"What were you doing so far out of goal, anyway?" another Barbarian scolded the goalkeeper.

The whistle for half-time sounded. The girls continued to quarrel while Alana's team celebrated. With the score at one-all, the home crowd was going wild. The three gorillas did star jumps. James hugged Jefri. Flynn and Sofia led a group of Gibbons supporters in a Mexican Wave.

"That is exactly what I'm talking about," Coach McNeeson beamed. "Gritty defense that's relentless. Relentless!" he cried. "You've rattled their cage, now. You've got them running scared. Now all you have to do is keep it up."

"Together," reminded Alana.

"Together," the other girls chorused.

The Barbarians didn't look like they were running scared, but they did look angry. One girl poked another in the chest and got poked back. Number 10 was blaming everybody and shouting, while Battle-Axe tried to break up a fight which had broken out between two others. The referee's whistle sounded.

"Is it too much to ask for you to win this thing?" Battle-Axe yelled as his team trooped back onto the field. "It's not like I'm asking you to donate a kidney!"

The girls on his team threw him a filthy look.

The Barbarians' Number 10 took off on her own again and after dribbling the ball past all of the Gibbons, took another shot at goal. It was a kick made under pressure though, and the angle was all wrong. Khalilah made a spectacular dive. To her relief, she managed to push it wide and it skimmed past the goal post. A second Barbarian made the same play, this time fending off her teammate, Number 10, as well. There was a lot of pushing and shoving between the two girls. In the end, the other Barbarian player fell as Number 10 took a vicious swipe at her legs. The ball rolled free of the pitch. The two girls exchanged furious words. Prita took the throw in and this time Alana headed the ball so that it dropped softly at her feet. Then she took off and danced around each of the Barbarians who tried to tackle her. They were fast and powerful, but she kept her feet light.

The music for the waltz snuck into her head and without thinking she began to hum and count. "One, two, three, dodge, one, two three, step back..."

She dove for the right. Number 10 was there, anticipating her, but it was a dummy move. Like a magician with a false sleight of hand, Alana sidestepped the outraged striker and then shot the ball through another player's legs, to catch up with the ball minutes later.

"That's a 'nutmeg'! The Falcons taught her that!" James told anybody who would listen.

Preyasi was wide open so Alana sent the ball across the field before running forward to collect it again on the return with a high kick that smashed the Barbarians' defense. The ball hit the top post and bounced on the goalkeeper's head before falling backward into goal. Score!

The crowd went ballistic.

The gorilla mascots replayed the move with kung fu kicks of their own. Jefri and Flynn began to waltz. Sofia did cartwheels while James caught flies with his mouth. The Falcons hadn't taught Alana *that* move and neither had James. Where had that ninja kick come from?

The Gibbons were now one up but the Barbarians fiercely protested the goal. "No! It's not fair!" Number 10 ranted, shadowing the referee at his every turn and getting into his face. The referee looked up, angry. Soon they were nose to belligerent nose. When several firm warnings didn't work, the referee thrust a yellow card into the air. "No way! You can't do that to me!" Number 10 protested. She turned and shoved her teammates aside before reaching over and burying her teeth in Khalilah's shoulder with a yell of frustration.

A shocked Khalilah screamed.

"What? I didn't do anything!" howled the Barbarian's Number 10. The half-moon holes in Khalilah's torn shirt told a different story.

Number 10 had earned a red card. Number 10 was off. The Barbarians were down one player.

"I can still play," Khalilah said, wincing. Her shoulder was already turning the color of grapes.

Coach McNeeson shook his head. It looked like he'd have to organize a tetanus shot. "You're up, Sofia," he called.

"But, but... they *bite*," she protested with wide eyes.

McNeeson looked at his watch. There wasn't much of the game left. "Don't worry. The biter's been sent off and your team will help defend the goal. We're up two-one, anyway. Anything we get now is a pure bonus," he assured her. "Believe me," he smiled, looking over at the other team, "Christmas for me has come early." Battle-Axe was giving the disgraced player a severe dressing down.

"Go Gibbons!" the Gibbons supporters screamed. "Go! Go! Go!"

With Number 10 on the bench, the rest of the Barbarians had a chance to share the play and moved the ball easily between them, despite being outnumbered. Before long, Sofia saw the ball coming toward her at what she calculated was 42 km/hour before pouncing on it with both arms and legs. Phew! Saved! But as she scrambled to get up, Sofia accidentally scissor-kicked the ball back into the goal in a move which sent the other team into paroxysms of delight. The score had equalized. Sofia covered her face in shame. An own goal! How could she be so stupid? "I suck!" she moaned. "I'm so sorry!" she told her teammates, but they had already resumed play.

Maddie touched the ball lightly to Alana who flicked the ball to Prita. Preyasi was ready to receive the ball as usual but the Barbarians were one step ahead of the twins and their player twirled in the air to block the shot. The ball bounced off her back with a force that sent the girl sprawling.

"I've got it. I've got it. I've got it," Sofia muttered to herself as the ball took a slow tumble toward her.

Sofia knew they didn't have much time. Sofia knew *she* didn't have much time to redeem herself. Sofia prayed to all the deities she could think of, but also reflected on a recent paper she'd read by Sandhu, Edgington, Grant, and Rowe-Gurney. According to their research, when a soccer ball is kicked, the distance that it bends is related to the ball's radius, the density of air, the ball's angular velocity, its velocity through the air, its mass, and the distance traveled by the ball in the direction it was kicked.

A picture of the equation floated into her brain:

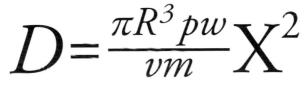

$$D = \frac{\pi R^3 pw}{vm} X^2$$

D: Distance a ball bends

R: Ball's radius

A: Density of air

E: Ball's angular velocity

V: Velocity through the air

M: Ball's mass

X: Distance traveled by ball in the direction it was kicked

"So if I do this," Sofia said to herself as she booted the ball back with all her might, "theoretically it should..."

Everybody watched it sail through the air. On and on and on, across the entire field! It almost landed directly into the other team's goal, but the Barbarian goalkeeper was ready and punched the ball up out of the way before running into the field, arms embracing the crowd. There was a collective groan from the Gibbons supporters.

The referee looked down at his watch.

"Yes!" The Barbarian goalie cried. "Yes! I did it!" There was no time for the Gibson Gibbons to get another goal in now. She closed her eyes and shook her fists into the air, victorious. The goalkeeper was so busy with self-congratulation that she missed her teammate's cries of panic and frantic hand signals. The kind of gestures that said: *"Behind you! The knife!"*

Only it wasn't a knife.

It wasn't even a hand drill.

It was something much, much worse.

Chapter 44

It was the ball bouncing back down once, twice, three times and rolling *backward* ever so slowly into goal.

The referee's whistle sounded.

The Gibson Gibbons had won.

CHAPTER 45

Dead body identified

Shall we check up on the body? Don't worry. It won't bite. Or not yet, anyway. *Mwa-ha-ha*. Forgive me. Death is not a time for jokes... *normally*. Fact: In the morgue they keep the temperature of bodies at 4 degrees Celsius. This slows down the rate of decomposition and keeps away the smell. Luckily, Sydney is bitter and cold this winter. The body is well preserved. That is not to say it is looking well, though. In fact, had the woman been alive, she would have dropped dead at the sight of herself. She would NEVER have chosen the conservative blue suit and orthopaedic shoes for any funeral, much less her own. Zsa Zsa Demure, or Mrs. Moira Cronenberg when she married, had more style and chutzpah than that.

The body –

Please, call me Moira.

When you see Moira standing at the bar of The Beauty Bar, you can understand Boris the

Imbécile's confusion. The stretch of timber has been converted into the reception where Katriona and Ling Ling write up appointments in a broad leather book in maroon. Moira is leaning back in a way she could never have done comfortably alive. While the wheelbarrow was handy delivering Moira this far, it did not help to maneuver her through the salon's narrow doorway, so Boris had to crank up one of her legs to squeeze her through. Rigor mortis makes the new pose permanent. Her arms remain by their side but one leg is bent at the knee. Much like the purple flamingo in Alana's living room. It suits her. Just as the new headdress with the fruit, tinsel, and three mini disco balls suits her. And the feather boa wrapped around her neck. Moira, propped up against the bar, looks like she is waiting for her own umbrella drink.

Moira will be missed. At the wake they will say that after seventy years – fifty years on stage, three divorces, one child, and a lifetime of ballroom dancing – it should not come to this. This standstill. That her body, now cold and quiet, should be so motionless. That she will never dance again. Or laugh at a bawdy joke. Or ignore her daughter's exasperated reprimands – "Do you really have to smoke, Mother? Do you really have to laugh so loud, Mother? Do you really have to wear those ridiculous outfits, Mother?"

Why yes. Yes I do. Because baby, like it or not, this is me. *What was it that poet, Khalil Gibran, said? "For what is it to die but to stand naked in the wind and to melt in the sun? And when the earth shall claim your limbs, then shall you truly dance."*

Moira is dancing. She may be dead, but she is still dancing.

CHAPTER 46

From the frying pan to the coffin?

Emma, Katriona and Ling Ling found the body in The Beauty Bar, after The Big Game became The Big Victory against the Bluejay Barbarians. The dead body was propped up against their counter, next to the catalogue display of "Summer's hot hues for hair." Ling Ling yelled an imprecation. "You said her name was Fok *Wee*," reminded Emma. Even though Ling Ling, had never met Fok Wee in person because all loans were made through an intermediary, everybody knew she was a little old lady who wore her hair in a top knot like a steamed bun balanced on top of her head, had skin as pale as milk, and teeth which were the best porcelain chompers money could buy. There was no doubt in Ling Ling's mind that the body in The Beauty Bar was Fok Wee Mung. If they lifted her eyelids, Ling Ling swore the woman's eyes would face different directions, like the all-seeing demon she was.

The shock of the discovery set their own bones in clay, so that when the phone rang, it was several minutes before they picked up. The call was a request for a last-minute hair appointment, and the client would be there in five. There was not enough time to do more than drag the body into the corner and shove the Salon Hood Hair Dryer, Model HB-M1028, over her head. Exactly five minutes later, the tinkle of the bell above The Beauty Bar's door announced the client's arrival. The client didn't notice the body, balancing like a flamingo in the corner of the room – perhaps because Katriona had assumed the pretence of painting the corpse's nails. Katriona chose a Liberace-inspired color called, Bling It On to match the feather boa. After all, just because the woman was dead, didn't mean it was the end of Style. As Ling Ling shampooed the client's hair, she longed to swap places with Katriona. Not because she particularly wanted to lacquer a dead woman's nails, but because under the bubbles of extra volume shampoo, *Judge Debnham* was pouring her heart out, as clients were wont to do.

Never had the three women jumped so quickly from the frying pan to the fire, or in this case, Ling Ling felt, a coffin. She didn't know the penalty for harboring a dead body in a beauty salon but she sensed it was *probably* worse than sixty hours of community service. Luck was on their side, however, and Judge Debnham's grief – *so sorry for your loss* – blinded her to the fact that the salon owners were Emma Oakley's friends from her "colorful past," that Emma Oakley herself (in a gorilla suit) was lying next to her at the shampoo basin, or that The Beauty Bar's other client was, in fact, dead.

Judge Debnham's hair was washed, primped, and curled in record time, so that she found herself outside The Beauty Bar door with ten minutes to spare and more tissues than she could use. "Such sweet beauticians," she sniffed. The sweet beauticians and Emma, meanwhile, were heaving the dead body up the stairs – careful, don't smudge her nails – and down a thick plank, through to next door's window. Arnie the Bodybuilder (and part-time political activist-slash-streaker) could cope with dead loan sharks better than they could...

Couldn't he...?

Five minutes later, Emma, Katriona, and Ling had a change of heart. It wasn't fair that Arnie should have to deal with their problem, even if the corpse was now rather cleverly disguised with a lampshade on her head. What they needed was concrete blocks on the dead woman's feet, a speedboat, and dark sunglasses. And maybe they should call each other names like Albert "the Executioner" Anastasia, Anthony "Gaspipe" Casso, and Louis "Louie Bagels" Daidone, suggested Emma, who was researching New York City Sicilian Mafia gangs for her latest article. While the trio redesigned the corpse's cement footwear, sorted out logistics, and argued who was going to be the *capo di tutti capi* or "Boss of Bosses," Arnie and a woman with fabulous-looking hair, strode through the door.

"What are you doing with my mother?!" Judge Debnham shrieked.

So. *Not* Fok Wee Mung after all.

Hmmm... *definitely* worse than sixty hours of community service.

CHAPTER 47

Missing persons

Alana Oakley noticed the missing wheelbarrow as soon as James dropped them home. Alana's senses tingled. The missing wheelbarrow and the missing body had to be linked – a fact confirmed by Mrs. Whetu next door, her graying hair still in rollers.

"Why, yes," Mrs. Whetu informed them with relish, "the skinny boy from across the road came looking for the mannequin from his mother's shop. Apparently it's missing. I told him I saw a body being carted out of your house last night in a wheelbarrow. By the boy in the leather jacket," she added, watching them closely.

For once, Alana was grateful for her nosy neighbor's powers of observation, and thanked Mrs. Whetu for the tip. Yes, she was helping the skinny boy from across the road recover the missing "mannequin," and no, she didn't know where the boy in the leather jacket was taking it, but she was sure it was all a big misunderstanding.

"You know how mixed up deliveries can get," Alana said pointedly, at which Mrs. Whetu's back stiffened – clearly Alana was onto her.

The four girls took off after the "mannequin" by following the tracks the wheelbarrow had left behind. Mud, paint, and even dog poo, had left a convenient, if somewhat smelly, trail. When the imprint left by the solitary wheel ran out, they asked nearby residents and passersby. They discovered people of Mrs. Whetu's ilk lived everywhere and helped them on their way. But now they were at a crossroads and had no idea which direction the body had gone.

Alana glanced at her watch. James would be picking them up soon for a celebratory dinner. They were running out of time.

"Why don't we call the delivery guy?" Maddie suggested.

"Of course!" Alana yelled. "You're brilliant!" Maddie dusted her shoulder and smiled.

But just up ahead, while Sofia tapped the number for Boris the Imbécile on her phone, Alana spotted a familiar figure. The boy had short, dark spiky hair, high cheekbones, and light-colored, deep-set eyes. It was Will, and by the look of it, he was searching for the body too!

What do you do when you have to confront a suspected vampire about your dead ballroom dancing teacher? *(Strategize! Call for reinforcements! Run!)*

Exactly! But that's *you*.

What Alana did was tackle.

"Where's Mrs. Cronenberg? What did you do to the dead body? Why did you turn her into a vampire?"

"Ummm, Alana," Maddie interrupted, "maybe Will could answer if you took the garlic out of his mouth."

Alana loosened her grip on Will's face and allowed him to spit out the bulb. He coughed and spluttered before picking bits of garlic from his teeth.

Will looked into Alana's eyes and Alana's throat closed up. His eyes. They were a rich, golden color. The color of liquid topaz. Like the eyes of a lion just before it opens up its maws to devour prey.

"You think I'm a *vampire*?" Will said.

Alana crossed her arms. "I *know* you are," and proceeded to list all of her suspicions against him and his family.

Will's answer to Alana's accusation was simple.

Plastic fangs – the kind from a joke shop – lay in the palm of his hand. *Will's always messing around. I'm sorry if he scared you.* Corinne Löfgren's voice echoed in Alana's head.

Alana refused to give up, although she did allow Will to sit. *Your pale skin?* We're half Swedish and Irish, what do you expect? *Steak tartare? Seriously? Who eats raw meat?* We do. *The Ouija board? How do you explain that?* I rigged it to spell "Woof." It was just a stupid joke. (But there was still the question of their ballroom dancing teacher. Dead the last time Alana saw her.) *And what was your dad doing with the body in your basement? Mrs.*

Cronenberg, wasn't it?

Will looked down and refused to meet their eyes. "Dad's a mortician," he admitted finally. "That means he prepares the deceased for viewing before their burial," he explained to Khalilah who didn't understand. Bruneian customs were very different. Dead bodies were wrapped in a shroud before being buried straight away. "We begged our parents not to tell anyone because people at our last school freaked. We don't even let Dad drive the hearse. He never brings his work home unless he has to, but sometimes it gets busy. Storage can get tight which is why Mom and Dad bought the house. Dad said the basement's perfect. Anyway," he continued, "Mrs. Cronenberg was another client. But she was the first one I knew personally. And the first to go missing."

Alana gave an uncomfortable cough.

"But of course, I would have jumped to the same conclusion. A vampire!" he chortled. "That's hilarious!"

"Yeah well somehow I don't think Katriona and

Ling Ling are going to think it's very funny," Sofia interrupted them. "Boris said he delivered the 'old bird' to The Beauty Bar half an hour ago."

Uh-oh!

The four friends and Will tore off down the street.

CHAPTER 48

To cut a long story longer

There was no easy answer to Judge Debnham's question ("What are you doing with my mother?!") without first explaining why Emma, Katriona, and Ling Ling were in Arnie's apartment. To do that, they had to start from the beginning.

"Katriona didn't want to celebrate her thirtieth birthday," Ling Ling began, "not even with paintball or a spa treatment or cake, and she kept saying, 'I'm nevereverevereverever getting out of bed!' and so she didn't, which made it impossible for me to run the business on my own, so I borrowed some money, and then we ran away because they wanted their money back, so when Katriona said she'd get out of bed to see Kylie Minogue in Tasmania, I jumped at the chance –"

"– but we couldn't take Emma's car because of, you know, what happened last time," Katriona continued, wisely not elaborating, "so she went to

Dodgy Dave's and got a Kombi van, but Ling Ling had to drive because Emma didn't feel confident in the new car. Then Emma put the wrong coordinates in the GPS, and we got lost in the desert somewhere –"

"– and we couldn't call anyone because Ling Ling packed everything except the phone charger and reception was so poor," Emma took up the story, "and when we *did* talk to someone, it was only my mother, so now I have to go to another cousin's wedding, with no date, as usual. And before that, Jinx got eaten by a snake, which we thought was a creepy bird and we went swimming in a billabong pool with crocodiles, and an alien spider attacked me, but luckily Katriona and Ling Ling killed it, and even luckier, a scientist found us and showed us where we could find a hotel, which..." Emma collapsed into giggles, "ended up being over the hill, only a few meters away. Funny, right?"

"Side-splitting," said Judge Debnham with no hint of a smile.

"And they even had the cute little umbrella drinks, remember?" Katriona reminded her.

"Yes," said Emma, "which made Katriona insanely happy, and then we saw the soccer game on TV, and that reminded me of Alana's game, so we hurried home as fast as we could, but Ling Ling chose the car with the giant mango on it, and actually..." Emma paused to think. "Maybe that's why the police were there? Maybe they wanted the mango back?"

Judge Debnham, having dealt with Emma before, was not surprised the police force was involved in the women's story. Trouble with a capital "T" didn't find Emma so much as hunt her down. Then just when the judge thought the day couldn't get any stranger, Emma's daughter, Alana, and four other teenagers climbed into her son's bedroom via the plank in the window. Shortly after came a boy in a leather jacket with the words "The Imbécile" embroidered on the back. The room was suddenly very crowded. A hail of voices started speaking at once.

"Wait one minute! Where do you think you're going with my mother?" Judge Debnham protested over the hubbub when she spied Boris maneuvering Moira out the window.

"The door. Good thinking," Boris said, as he and the corpse did an about-face.

"Oh no, you're not," Judge Debnham said, pulling on her mother.

"Oh yes, I am," insisted Boris. C.O.D. meant Cash On Delivery and Boris was yet to deliver.

Alana interceded before the tug-of-war split Mrs. Cronenberg in two, and explained to Boris that the "blue bird" he was supposed to deliver was still back at her house. To Judge Debnham, she explained that Mr. Löfgren had outsourced the hair and makeup to The Beauty Bar for authentic "Showbiz Pizzazz."

Emma, Ling Ling, and Katriona nodded vigorously after only *two* sharp elbows in the ribs.

"Because," Alana said, taking a punt on her powers of observation, "you know Mrs. Cronenberg wouldn't really be happy in that suit, or those orthopedic shoes." Alana said the word "orthopaedic" as if it was toe jam or something, and Judge Debnham nodded against her will. All the fight seemed to flow out of her body and she leaned on Arnie's arm for support. Ling Ling hoped Judge Debnham wouldn't start crying again. She was out of tissues.

Then Judge Debnham made one last attempt to assert her authority. Weren't there a hijacked mango and a stolen car the women had to answer for? At which point Ling Ling reminded the judge in a whisper of her son's weekend political activities and a certain tattoo as proof, should it be required. Aloud, Judge Debnham assured them smoothly that it wasn't necessary. Mangoes went missing all the time and it was easy enough to choose the wrong car in the dark. Public funds were better spent elsewhere.

"We should go free Tibet together, some time," Katriona purred in an aside to Arnie. The bodybuilder leaned into the wall away from her.

Chapter 48

...

It would be nice to say that that was the end of little old ladies turning up dead in this story, but it wouldn't be true.

Fok Wee Mung was still hot on Ling Ling's heels, and it was a debt she decided to collect in person...

CHAPTER 49

Love triangle

A thumb, gnarled and knotted with arthritis, stroked a black and white photograph with tenderness. Nobody would have recognized the sweet face in the picture to be Fok Wee Mung, wedged between a much younger, handsome dark-haired boy and an Italian beauty. Fok Wee Mung had known love firsthand, but for her there had been no happy ending. The boy had dumped Fok Wee Mung for the Italian beauty in the photo (!) and then left the Italian for a different girl months later. But not before giving Fok Wee's present to him, to his Italian girlfriend. Fok Wee Mung was so hurt she felt as if he'd knocked her down with a bus and then reversed over her with a semitrailer. That was *Fok Wee's* leather jacket, embroidered with *her* nickname. She was the "Crazy Mother," not the Italian! Fok Wee Mung resisted the urge to crumple up the snapshot as a familiar wave of hatred washed over her, feeling a sense of triumph for not doing so. She was strong.

When Fok Wee Mung's driver and lackey finished parking the black, vintage Jaguar opposite The Beauty Bar on King Street, he expected to be sent out to do his "duty" without delay. That was what usually happened. He was the family's only heir after all, and it was part of the family's business to steam buns in the morning and collect debts in the afternoon. Truth be told, Fok Jun Mung preferred molding dough to mashing faces, a fact he hid from his mother, who he always thought of as, well, a bit crazy. Nobody was more surprised than he when, without warning, his mother jumped out of the car and rushed out in the middle of King Street's traffic.

Fok Wee Mung's heart was in her mouth when she spotted the boy in the leather jacket through the tinted glass of the car. The boy made his way toward The Beauty Bar with a slouch and a swagger she instantly recognized. Was it him? Could it be? But no, she thought. He would be in his sixties by now. Whoever he was, he was the spitting image of him. Fok Wee Mung reached out her hand to the love of her life as if in a dream. She stepped forward. Her vision strained in her +4.0 lens tortoiseshell glasses as she struggled to read. *It's...*

The Imbécile??!

...

"Cardiac arrest" was the official finding of the coroner who presided over the post-mortem of the seventy-eight-year-old female known as Fok Wee Mung. This was of great comfort to the bus driver who thought it was because he'd knocked Fok Wee Mung over. But it was of less comfort to the soft-hearted driver of the semitrailer truck who had followed through.

Boris the Imbécile had no idea his father had been the love of Fok Wee Mung's life, or that his dad's departure had been the source of Fok Wee's life lived in bitterness. After all, Boris' father had left him too, well before he'd been born. All he had to remember him by was an old leather jacket with the words "Crazy Mother" embroidered on the back. Boris felt proud of the new name he'd had embroidered. "The Imbécile" sounded much more macho than the original.

Of even greater interest to the hundreds of people in debt to the late Fok Wee Mung was that Fok's Bakery changed its name to Big Money, and thereafter dedicated itself to a life without crime and a new product line: fortune cookies.

CHAPTER 50

Drop-dead gorgeous

Shall we take a final look at the body? Sequins, frills, feathers, rhinestones. It is the grandest ensemble of Corinne Löfgren's career. And The Beauty Bar's hair, nails, and makeup are the perfect compliment. Moira Cronenberg shimmers and shines as she stands – stands! – like a Greek goddess, one knee bent slightly, chin tilted imperiously as she stretches out an arm, waiting for an invisible dance partner. The sight of her makes some funeral guests catch their breath... and others choke on their puff pastries.

The funeral parlor is stripped of all references to religion. There are no crosses, no angels, no hints of an afterlife. The stained glass windows are abstract slivers of sparkling color that allude to roses, violets, and lilies. At the oak door entrance, Vlad Löfgren welcomes each guest with a solemn shake of the hand. A conciliatory bow.

His eyes are warm with sympathy. He is careful not to smile. He knows his teeth make people feel uncomfortable. Vlad accepts the compliments for Moira's final "look" with grace and humility. The decision to allow Moira to remain standing to honor her final memory and true spirit is a bold and unconventional one. He hears one guest murmur, "Moira looks like she belongs in a wax museum." Her partner disagrees, "No, she looks like she belongs on the stage."

Vlad Löfgren is no stranger to unusual requests. Last week he presided over a dead clown. The clown was buried in full costume, from the red nose to the oversized boots (this was a problem when they tried to put the lid on). The makeup took Vlad two full days to get right. When they arrived, the family was dressed as clowns. The guests dressed as clowns. In keeping with the family's request, Vlad and his colleagues were clowns too. A tiny, blue teardrop was painted beneath everybody's eye.

Over fifty sad clowns, each marked with a solitary tear.

After shaking Vlad Löfgren's hand, the guests pay their respects to Judge Debnham who in contrast to her mother is dressed in a black veil and Trent Nathan suit. Her son, Arnold – no need to change his nickname – is in Valentino. Arnold pulls at his collar as if he is choking. His bodybuilder's frame stretches the fabric so that he looks like Bruce Banner seconds before he turns into The Hulk. People mistake him for his mother's bodyguard and they look past him to comment on the flower arrangements and the weather. Judge Debnham welcomes her mother's friends with a straight back. Their kind words and sympathetic cooing reminds her of pigeons. She nods as she accepts their condolences. The mood is fittingly somber.

Judge Debnham glances over at her mother and feels her heart tighten. Sequins, frills, feathers, rhinestones. Moira Cronenberg is a glittering monument to a life lived passionately through dance. No, she realizes. This is not how it should be. This is not how Moira Cronenberg, nee Zsa Zsa Demure, would like it to end.

Chapter 50

Judge Debnham, to the astonishment of the celebrant, the guests, her own son, Arnold, and herself most of all, makes an announcement:

"My mother used to say, 'Dance is to touch. To move. To inspire'. Dance is what made my mother happiest, and boy, could that woman dance." The guests give a low, appreciative chuckle. " 'Never miss a chance to dance, Martha,' she told me, and it was a philosophy she herself lived by. Even when she could no longer perform on stage, she kept dancing and passing on her love of dance to a younger generation." Judge Debnham looks at Alana and her classmates who have come to pay their respects. Her eyes soften. "I cannot imagine anything which would make her smile more than us taking this chance to dance at her funeral. So," Judge Debnham says, holding out her hand to her son, Arnold, who takes it, completely bemused, "this one is for you, Zsa Zsa." And Martha Debnham and her son, Arnold, lead the others in a waltz, and then a jig, as Maddie picks up the tempo on her violin.

CHAPTER 51

Thinking big

The Year Ten Formal or spring dance was all the middle school of Gibson High could talk about and the buzz of excitement made it impossible for students to concentrate on work. Not that work was a major concern anymore. The mid-year exams were over and the promise of warmer weather chased the final ghouls of winter and solemnity from the classrooms. To Alana, it felt as if everybody was going to the dance except her. Khalilah, Maddie, and Flynn were in the classical orchestra to perform, and even Sofia was going to go as Jefri's "date." Sofia was thrilled, even though they were being chaperoned by Mrs. Madzaini and a visiting aunt arriving from Brunei.

"We're just friends," Jefri kept reassuring Miller.

It didn't help Alana's mood that her mom was involved in the preparations too. Alana suspected she'd been shamed into it by their neighbor, Corinne Löfgren, who had let slip that she was organizing the decorations, in between running her shop and volunteering at the local hospice, and would Mrs. Oakley like some home-baked apple pie?

No, Emma refused with a tight smile, and then set about organizing the entertainment for the dance after putting a call through to James. He has a million and one contacts, Emma assured Alana, and if he doesn't, she faltered, thinking about the Elvis Convention she covered every year, I know a couple of people.

And so the ball was sent rolling...

Have you got a picture of the ball in your mind?

Make it bigger.

Now make it bigger again.

Keep making the ball bigger until it gets *Raiders of the Lost Ark* big and it's chasing you, Harrison Ford and the little kid, Short Round, down. *Now* you're in the right frame of mind for what is about to happen, because even if you or

I have forgotten, and maybe even Alana, Emma still has plans for her daughter's 15th birthday. According to her, it's the Best One Yet.

CHAPTER 52

Cinderella

On the first of September, Alana's home was a flurry of makeup and underwear and hair product as Khalilah, Maddie, and Sofia rushed from bathroom to mirror to bedroom to get ready for the dance. Khalilah and Maddie were dressed in ruffled white shirts and black trousers for the classical orchestra, and were fussing over Sofia. Sofia had bought her outfit from Revamped, a floor-length dress cut on the bias with thin shoulder straps and long flowing lines. A silk scarf in orange trimmed with tiny brass medallions was the perfect foil for Sofia's electric blue dreads which were now almost to her knees. She was so happy with what Corinne Löfgren had designed; the strategic cuts in the fabric showed off her belly piercing perfectly! Alana put her new skills into play and expertly retouched Sofia's eyeliner which had smudged.

"Are you sure you don't want to work at The Beauty Bar full time?" Maddie asked with a cheeky grin after inspecting Sofia in the mirror. "You'd get a job, for sure."

Alana shook her head. Their "success" at the funeral had revived The Beauty Bar's reputation and they were busier than ever. Alana had been recruited to do Thursday nights and Saturday mornings on top of her holiday work, but that was more than enough for her. She didn't want another talk with Mr. Turner about failing to meet scholarship requirements, and if she was right about the mid-term exams, she shouldn't have to. Alana couldn't help feeling a little bit like Cinderella, though, as everyone got ready for the "ball." Although the thought of dancing in public was utterly abhorrent, she would have liked the chance to hang out with her friends. That the dance coincided with her birthday made it suck even more. Everybody was so busy getting ready that her friends hadn't even remembered. Even her mom was too preoccupied to make the usual fuss.

Maybe her birthday wasn't going to be a disastrous extravaganza this year? Maybe, it wasn't even going to happen!

But it was too much to hope for, Alana realized, as soon as everyone yelled, "Surprise!" and handed her a present, eyes gleaming with excitement: a necklace from Khalilah, a bracelet from Sofia, hair accessories from Maddie, a pair of high heels from Katriona and Ling Ling (absent because they were fully booked that night), and a dress from Revamped from her mom, who was grinning in that crazy way that showed her gums and made her eyes disappear. Alana noticed a distinct theme to this year's birthday presents...

Was Cinderella going to the ball after all?

Alana recalled Emma's note from months before: *P.S. I've sorted out that problem you were telling me about and the new neighbors are ecstatic to help. I won't say anymore because I don't want to spoil the surprise but I can't WAIT for your birthday!* The debacle with Mrs. Cronenberg had proved that Emma had not asked the Löfgrens to help get rid of Alana's ballroom dancing teacher, as Alana first assumed, which could only mean that ...

Blart! Blart! Blart!

What could be a worse birthday present than having to kickbox your P.E. teacher or for your hair to catch fire?

Will "Fangs" Löfgren.

The Year Ten Formal.

Will's dad's *company car.*

CHAPTER 53

The ball

Alana agreed to everything – unwillingly and ungraciously – everything, except the heels.

"I'm already going to fall flat on my face," she grumbled. "I don't need help from these." She held the dainty slippers that winked and sparkled in the light, as if they were covered in manure. Khalilah whipped them off Alana's fingers and wailed when they didn't fit. What kind of diet helped you lose weight on your *feet*?

"You look really gorgeous, Lala," Emma sniffed, tears making her dark, brown eyes appear glassy. "So grown up. And the boots give it some real –"

"– edge," said Sofia. "You look perfect."

Alana snuck a look at her reflection in the mirror. Khalilah had used a straightener to tame the natural kink in Alana's hair. Maddie's chocolate eyeliner made Alana's eyes look smoky and huge. Sofia touched up the lip gloss which made Alana's lips look full and shiny. The dress Corinne Löfgren had made for Alana was fashioned from T-shirt and tulle. Corinne was given a couple of old outfits that Alana had outgrown and reworked it in a new style with velvet, silk, and leather. It shouldn't have worked. None of it. And yet it did.

"Not everyone can rock that look," Khalilah said. Her two friends nodded in agreement.

Alana turned to face her 15th birthday with squared shoulders and a glint to her eye that would have made any firing squad think twice.

"Bring it on!" she said.

Everybody laughed. "Take it easy, Drama Queen," mocked Maddie, "it's only the Year Ten Formal."

CHAPTER 54

A dance to remember

Everybody admired the decorations for the formal which sparkled and shone. Corinne Löfgren had done a spectacular job with this year's theme of a "Star-Studded Occasion" and Gibson High's Hall on the top floor glimmered like the cave of a dragon's hoard. A plush, red carpet strip led guests to a compact dance floor of polished timber. To the left was a large stage for the classical orchestra and to the right was a sumptuous buffet table smothered in tempting goodies.

"Not for us," Maddie warned Khalilah when her feet took off in the wrong direction. "Not yet, anyway." The two of them joined the others on stage to tune their instruments. Flynn was already there but jumped down the minute he spotted Alana.

"Save a dance for me, Oakley," he said, to

which Alana could only manage a garbled reply. She was still recovering from the ride in the hearse. Sofia, Maddie, and Khalilah had shot into the rear of the car without hesitation, lying down where the coffin would have been, all three of them in a fit of giggles. That's weird, thought Alana, until she noticed them doing a pantomime through the window with gruesome masks and gory Halloween props. No wonder passersby had given her such odd looks!

A harried-looking Emma startled Alana out of her day-mare. "Have you seen James?"

"No," Alana said. "Why?"

"He said the Stars were confirmed for tonight, but they still haven't arrived," Emma moaned. "It looks like we'll have to improvise."

"Mooooom!" Alana said, fear lacing her voice, but Emma was already gone. The first notes of the waltz began.

Alana was thankful to Flynn for his impromptu dance lessons, as was Will who secretly wore three pairs of socks under the steel-capped shoes bought especially for the occasion. Alana stepped lightly – or as lightly as she could in her boots – to the sweeping sounds created by her friends in the orchestra. If she turned her head quickly she could see them on stage. Flynn winked as he blew on his saxophone, gray eyes watching her every move. Maddie's grin was huge. She had scored her precious "chair" and Alana had never seen her so happy or proud. Khalilah swung her flute excitedly, to the dismay of Miss Beatrice who was conducting, and on the dance floor, Sofia waved as she whirled past.

And then it was over.

Nine months of stress for four measly minutes! Alana thought sourly. Maddie was right. You had to be careful what you wished for. Alana couldn't wait to get back to "normal" P.E.

"James?" Emma's frantic voice cut through the excited babble as Alana and her friends clustered around the buffet table cradling brightly colored mocktails and plates of finger food. Emma disappeared for a second time, speaking frantically on her phone, before Alana could finish shaking her head.

"That reminds me," said Khalilah. "Where are Mom and Auntie Nor? They should be here by now."

Jefri looked around the hall but could see neither of his relatives who were supposed to be chaperoning them for the night.

"Maybe they got held up," Will said with a smirk, and gave an exaggerated bow inviting Sofia to dance.

Alana narrowed her eyes at Will while her friends returned to the stage. Will may not be a vampire but he was definitely Up To Something. Before Alana could give it another thought, though, Jefri was leading her in another head-spinning waltz.

CHAPTER 55

Perfect timing

Alana was right. Will was Up To Something. Or he had been. Will Löfgren loved to play pranks, as the vampire fangs and Ouija board could attest to, so when he spied an Out-of-Order sign on the school's service elevator, he couldn't resist taking it down. It was a harmless enough joke. Nobody but the catering staff used the elevator, anyway. Or so he thought.

Ten minutes later, Dr. Nicolette Luciano, Mrs. Amal Madzaini, and her sister, Nor, smiled their thanks at the woman who held the service elevator doors open. Amal and Nor could not have looked more different. Both women wore their headscarves for the occasion but where Amal's face was open and warm, Nor's face was stern and disapproving. As Sofia confided to Alana: "She's the scariest-looking nun I've ever seen." Behind them, an older woman grumbled at an elderly man like a farmer harassing a wayward donkey.

"I told you to stay at home. You and your bunged up knee. Maddie'll be done before we even get there," she griped.

"There's a lift, Auntie Mo and Uncle Joe," the woman in the elevator called out. She gave Dr. Luciano, Mrs. Madzaini, and Nor an apologetic smile for the delay.

After several more minutes of good-natured bickering and painstaking shuffling, the elderly pair joined the others in the elevator. The doors closed with a clunk and a grind and began a shuddering ascent that stopped abruptly midway.

"Maximum weight: 1,740 kilograms," Auntie Mo squinted. "See, I knew you shoulda never-a come."

Uncle Joe made an attempt to suck in his stomach which lasted five seconds before flopping over the waistband of his dress trousers. Nancy Dawson gave the number one button several more jabs. Amal Madzaini and her sister, Nor, exchanged worried glances. Nancy smiled reassuringly although concern clouded her aquamarine eyes. With a triumphant shout, Auntie Mo spotted the answer to their troubles and punched the red emergency button so hard it fell to the ground.

Everybody's backs stiffened.

"He-he, don't know me own strength," Auntie Mo muttered.

"I do," Uncle Joe piped up.

Auntie Mo aimed a swift mock blow at Uncle Joe's bicep to shut him up. *See?* His wounded expression seemed to say.

"Should we try the phone?" Nicolette Luciano interrupted. She could feel the walls collapsing in on them, the smell of stale cigarette butts and pine forest cleanser hung thick in the air. But the box where the phone should have been was empty, and nobody's mobile phone could get reception.

After half an hour of yelling and banging on the doors, the five of them settled down for a long wait. Pretty soon it was revealed that Nicolette was Sofia's mom, Nancy Dawson was Maddie's, and

Amal was Khalilah's. Although their girls were best friends, had often stayed at each other's houses, and the adults had even spoken on the phone, none of them had met until now. The conversation twisted and turned from school work to music practice and then the trials of bringing up a teenager.

"I don't know what garbage they're feeding them these days." Auntie Mo sniffed. "All this fairytale nonsense."

"Oh, yes," Nicolette agreed, "Sofia's utterly obsessed with those romance books, the ones where the human girl, vampire, and werewolf are caught in a love triangle."

"My Khalilah, too," Amal revealed.

"Romantic love," Nancy sighed with a roll of her eyes.

The women warmed to their topic as they spoke about books and overrated love and unrealistic expectations. Real Love, they said, was the warts and flaws left behind when the Fairytale Love of hearts, flowers, and happy-ever-afters had faded. How could the girls possibly know what Real Love was? They were like tadpoles looking up through the water and imagining life as a frog. They didn't even have legs, and yet they wanted to jump through the air! *Yes, yes.* They agreed. *Yes!* Uncle Joe tuned out the babble by flicking off his hearing aid and settling down for a nap.

"They puke, they snore, they fart," Auntie Mo said, repeating her favorite mantra with crossed arms, "and the sooner they realize it, the better!"

On cue, Uncle Joe's backside erupted with such ferocious intent he woke himself up. To his astonishment, when he opened his eyes he saw all four women screaming and bashing the elevator doors with renewed vigor. Tears streamed from their eyes.

"Must've been some explosion," he muttered, checking all his limbs were present and accounted for. "'s okay, ladies," he assured them, "I'm alright."

CHAPTER 56

A ball like no other

Mr. Turner, the deputy principal and acting head, made his speech to the Year Tens and their parents and teachers, who were assembled in the school hall. As Year Seven students, he reminisced, they were encouraged to "explore, experiment and enjoy." Now, a mere four years later, he was sending them off to be the best they could be, to fulfill their potential and to create their own path with the tools the school had given them. Not all of the students would continue their studies at Gibson High. Some would graduate and take up apprenticeships or attend community colleges or go overseas as part of the foreign exchange program with partner schools. "Be the change that you want to see in the world," Mr. Turner advised with his arms outstretched, "and you will create a world of change."

Emma looked around nervously. Most of Mr. Turner's speech was going over her head, not least because she was distracted by his looks. Over the years Mr. Turner had grown even more portly and his beard had turned puffy and white. She half expected him to erupt with a "Ho ho ho!" even though Christmas was three months away. Beards. Hmmm. With November coming up, she could do a piece on the Movember Foundation that funded men's health programs... Emma jotted down a couple of ideas on the tablecloth and made a mental note to sneak it home later. She noted with dismay that tonight's nail art was totally ruined. Emma's fingernails had been bitten to the quick. She didn't want to admit it but NONE of the evening's entertainment had turned up! She certainly wasn't saying anything to Corinne Löfgren who was basking in the praise of the Parent-Teacher Committee members like a gecko soaking up the sun. James assured her that they were on the way, possibly stuck in traffic, Newtown *was* notorious for it, but it didn't stop

Emma racing backward and forward so much she'd made a groove in the red carpet. She was running out of time.

Thank goodness Emma had the Elvis Convention organizer on speed dial!

In the meantime, Emma asked Katriona and Ling Ling to be on the lookout for the Stars, and to direct them backstage as soon as they arrived. The classical orchestra had already cleared the stage of all their instruments and DJ Yama was ready to finish the night off. If only the Stars would arrive to fill in the middle!

The sound of polite applause heralded the end of Mr. Turner's speech and he searched the sea of faces for Emma to introduce the next item on tonight's agenda: the Entertainment. Emma squared her shoulders, walked up the stairs and took the microphone from him with a frozen smile. There was no choice but to use Plan B.

"Welcome everybody," she said. Emma's voice broke midway and she cleared her throat longer than necessary to buy some time. "First of all, I'd like to thank Corinne Löfgren for the incredible job she has done transforming the Gibson High School Hall. What a stunning job, Corinne. Simply stunning." The audience clapped and yelled as Corinne hid her head in Will's shoulder. "And speaking of 'stunning,' I want to take this opportunity to wish my 'stunning' daughter a Happy Birthday! Happy birthday, Alana!"

Alana's face flamed as Flynn blew the first few notes of Happy Birthday on his saxophone while her friends clapped and cheered.

"You know, fifteen years ago, if you had've told me that this tiny, cute little bundle with rosy cheeks and hair, oh my gosh, so much hair, well, I thought, no wonder my tummy was so big, she practically had a mohawk when she came out..." Emma's arms flung high to demonstrate.

Alana buried her face in her hands. "Make her stop," she moaned as Emma began reliving Alana's childhood that began with a difficult birth. Almost as if he had heard her, Mr. Turner stepped forward halfway through a story on Alana's potty training, and whispered into Emma's ear.

"Oh yes," said Emma, "our entertainment. Our entertainment for tonight's theme of a Star-Studded Occasion is FULL of Stars. In fact, it has so many Stars that we should have called it a *Galaxy*-Studded Occasion!" Emma's laughter was high-pitched and forced. She laughed again, and then snorted. And then laughed because she'd snorted. And then laughed again. "I'm sorry," she said to the audience who were now staring at their feet or away. "I always make that awful sound when I'm nervous." Alana's expression was bleak.

An urgent *Psst!* off-stage finally caught Emma's attention and what she saw turned her feet to stone. Emma wasn't quite sure if she believed in reincarnation. She was even less committed to the idea of zombies. But if she did prescribe to either or both, she could have sworn Mrs. Moira Cronenberg, nee Zsa Zsa Demure, was back!

The figure was short and stocky. The faint line of fuzz that sat above the painted rosebud mouth had been plastered over with foundation and dusted with powder. Long, fake eyelashes framed a pair of hazel green eyes. Ruffles, oodles of them, hung off the person's white, pudgy shoulders and wrapped themselves around their body like a spiral staircase. The headpiece was a glittering tower of plastic jewels and fake curls. It was a figure you expected to drawl, "Dah-ling!" before air-kissing the side of your face, three times. *It* was definitely star-studded. "Mrs. Moira Cronenberg" ghosted forward to take the microphone from Emma, who managed a squeaky "Let the show begin!" before staggering off the stage.

"At first I was afraid, I was terrified. Kept thinking I could never live without you by my side..." Colin Johnson's voice started out faint and shaky, but gained strength when someone in the audience gave an appreciative hoot. Here was Colin Johnson – the Year Nine boy known to be more comfortable with a drawing pencil or a joystick in his hand ... and now a dress.

An Elvis joined Colin on stage. And then another. And another. Soon the stage was full of them. There was Aloha-jumpsuit Elvis. Gold-lamé-tuxedo Elvis. Red-matador-suit Elvis, and Rhinestone-cape Elvis. Elvis with sideburns. Elvis with slicked hair. Elvis with flares. As the disco beat pumped its rhythm, the Stars on stage belted out the seventies classic with so much zeal and verve, it was impossible for the Year Tens to resist. *So retro!* they nodded to each other like ostriches. *Wicked!*

Katriona and Ling Ling stood outside the doors of the school hall, trying to direct the flood of Elvises in the right direction. Two figures caught their attention immediately. They were not an Elvis, but as impersonators, they looked almost as good.

"Name?" Katriona asked, checking the list Emma had given her.

A petite woman answered with a hint of a smile in her voice. "Kylie. Kylie Minogue."

"No, no. Not who you've come as. Your real name," Katriona said.

"My real name *is* Kylie Minogue."

A voice piped up beside her. It belonged to a vision of otherworldliness -- an Amazon of a woman with regal bearing and piercing, blue eyes behind a pair of glittering, curlicue-shaped eyeglasses. She looked like a multihued butterfly emerging from an opera-house-inspired chrysalis – if the butterfly weighed eighty kilograms. Sharp blue eyes narrowed as they took in Katriona's deplcted halter neck and swollen bell bottoms. "She *really is* Kylie Minogue, Possum."

Katriona rolled her eyes at Ling Ling who shrugged. Katriona was sick of the fake Elvises, their rocking pelvises, and their well-a, well-a, huhs. They'd both had a long day on their feet at The Beauty Bar. Was it too much to ask for a straight answer to a straight question? But no, here was another one giving her a hard time.

Katriona looked the woman up and down. "So, you're the *real* Kylie Minogue?" Two pairs of scathing digits encompassed the word "real."

The petite woman nodded.

"Well, there's an easy way to prove that!"

...

When Jefri saw two women stride angrily past him on his way back from the bathroom, heading straight for the service elevator, his neck turned like it was made of rubber. He recognized both of them from his book, *Australian Icons*.

"Tipu!" Lies, he cried. "I knew it was all real!"

The *ding* of the elevator heralded its arrival. It discharged Dr. Nicolette Luciano, Mrs. Amal Madzaini, Nor, Auntie Mo, and ... an ungodly smell. The four women pushed past Jefri, coughing and spluttering and wildly batting at the air, as if they could *punch* the smell away. When the stench reached the two women waiting for the service elevator, they clutched at each other with glazed eyes, before staggering blindly for the stairs.

"What did I miss?" said Uncle Jo, emerging through the doors with a slow shuffle as he turned up his hearing aid. "What did I miss?"

...

Back in the school hall, with all Elvises present and accounted for, Katriona and Ling Ling and Emma led the others in shaking their bootie and jabbing their fingers in the air. Even though it was a little bit late in coming, Katriona couldn't have asked for a better birthday present.

Her friends had managed to Turn Back Time.

CHAPTER 57

Happy never after

All things considered, Alana was quite happy with the way her 15th birthday was turning out. True, Emma had embarrassed her in front of all her friends and the seniors at the school ball. True, Emma had forced Alana to ride to school in a hearse, and true, she'd been made to dance the waltz in public. But Alana wasn't in hospital and more importantly, Coach Kusmuk was nowhere to be seen. Plus DJ Yama was playing some wicked beats that, even though they weren't rock, weren't bad. Thanks to Flynn, Alana's mind was now open to a whole new world of music... even if she drew the line at Tom Waits.

"Miss you, Dad," Alana aimed at the glittery ceiling in a whisper, imagining him with his frizzy hair, acoustic guitar, and tender smile before he blew her a birthday kiss.

The track changed suddenly to reflect Alana's melancholic mood. The frantic beats shifted to something unhurried and gentle: a slow dance that forced the hordes to sway somewhat stupidly to the music, or surrender the dance floor to couples.

Alana looked around to find Khalilah communing with the desserts table. Maddie and Jefri were congratulating Colin. Sofia was schmoozing it with Will. She'd been abandoned by everyone except Flynn, who stood in front of her, shirt buttoned wrongly as usual, hair an unkempt mess, and eyes, two fathomless pools.

"So," he said, stepping forward, "you did good, Oakley."

"I had a good teacher," Alana said, taking a step forward, too. "Well, 'good' might be an exaggeration."

One more step and there would be no space between them.

"When are you going to learn that it doesn't get any better than me?" Flynn said, all trace of humor gone.

Alana shot him a look that would have melted Medusa herself, but Flynn had thick skin and remained standing.

One more step and there would be no space between them.

Alana wondered whether she should ride her bike home. She wondered if she had seaweed stuck between her teeth. She wondered how old you should be for your first kiss.

One more step and there would be no space between them.

Alana bent her head and noticed there was no more space between them. She looked up...

... *at her mom, Emma?*

"Hi Alana, Flynn, are you having a good time? Goodness, for a minute I thought it was going to be a com-plete disaster, but it just goes to show, you never know."

Alana stepped back. The moment lost.

"And everybody loved those stories of you! I didn't even get to tell them that funny one about the bed-wetting. Remember that one, darling? You were so cute when you were little! Oops, excuse me, I *must* say thank you to Colin..." Emma hurried past them both.

Alana took another step back. Away from Flynn's smiling eyes and barely contained laughter. She'd known in her bones that her birthday had been too good to be true. That she was crazy to think she could get away with mere public humiliation. At least it was only Flynn.

"Careful not to drink too much before bedtime, Alana," said a familiar voice. "We wouldn't want to have an 'accident,' would we?" With a sinking feeling, Alana turned to face Coach Kusmuk. Kusmuk pretended to lower her voice as she gestured toward Alana's mouth, "And you've got a bit of uh, seaweed, stuck between your teeth."

CHAPTER 58

A fairy-tale ending

Alana's lips were not the only ones left unkissed. Cassy Dawson, Maddie's little sister, was still pretending to be Snow White on her makeshift bed of paper blossoms. She was still waiting for a kiss from her prince. And she was still waiting for him, even as her eyes closed and the letters in her favorite book turned blurry, so that she almost missed it when it happened. Quick as lightning and as gentle as a butterfly.

"Night night, Princess."

Cassy's eyes flew open and her arms were around her father's neck even before she'd woken up. She knew her wish would come true!

There was lots of noise then, the kind of burbling chatter that always accompanies late night cups of tea and catch-up conversations. Troy ached to tell his dad about school. Maddie had news about her violin performance at the school dance, and Cassy insisted on reading him a story.

"Read?" Auntie Mo scoffed. "Her scrawny butt hasn't left that bed since you left," she informed the trucker who was placidly sipping a cup of tea, one arm around Maddie's mom, Nancy. "It doesn't count just because you've memorized it," she said to Cassy.

Cassy stood up and shot Mo a look that Mo herself was impressed with, but didn't dare show it. She snatched a random white envelope from the coffee table and ripped it open.

"Dear Miss Madison Dawson, Congratulations. Your application to Sydney's Conservatorium High School has been successful. Please contact the Admissions Office for further information. We wish you all the best. Sincerely, Professor Tane Rangi." Cassy's narrow shoulders shook as she tried to catch her breath.

"Are you sure there's not an 'un' after the word 'successful,' Cassy?" Maddie said faintly.

"No. I'm very sure," Cassy said belligerently.

"Me and my scrawny butt *can* read."

Nobody knew how to react. Everything felt like it was tumbling around inside, as twisted as a car wreck. Maddie took the letter from Cassy gently.

"Cassy. You can read."

"Yes." Cassy's eyes widened. "Maddie. You're going away to study."

"Sounds like it."

Then the words started to fly around the room with more urgency. Cassy-can-read-Maddie-Sydney-Conservatorium-I-don't-believe-it-Cassy-Maddie-Cassy ... Under the table, slightly away from the shouting and screaming, Cassy crawled over to Troy to stare at him with big, serious eyes.

"I can come to school now." She paused, thinking that maybe it was safer to ask. "Is that okay with you?"

Troy's face broke into a huge grin. "Yeah! I can teach you to jump and you can teach me to read!"

CHAPTER 59

Opportunity knocks

Several suburbs away in the Madzaini household, voices were also being raised but not in joy.

"I don't understand why I have to go *now*," Khalilah said to the three adults sitting on the couch. "I'm happy here, and Mama hasn't finished her PhD yet."

Auntie Nor sniffed in annoyance. "We have a family tradition of going to the U.K. for our education. Sometimes it is after your high school graduation. If you are very fortunate, sometimes it is before. This is a golden opportunity to attend one of the most prestigious ladies colleges in the world. I, myself, went there. You will learn proper manners, deportment, etiquette, the right way to speak..."

"What's wrong with the way I speak?" Khalilah pouted.

Auntie Nor's lips pressed together so thinly they almost disappeared as Jefri sashayed through the living room and up the stairs, urging people to "do the Locomotion." She did not want to tell Khalilah the real reason for moving her to the exclusive, all-girl's boarding school. Jefri might be a lost cause but Khalilah at least, was still young enough to be molded into someone suitable for society. If her wayward sister, Amal, didn't want to think about their social position, then it was up to Nor to take matters into her own hands. "This is what you've said you've always wanted."

Khalilah looked momentarily confused. "I did. I mean I do. I just thought I'd go there for university, or something. That I'd have more time here." Khalilah looked at her parents, clearly distressed. "I've made such good friends."

Amal quickly jumped in before her older sister could tell Khalilah unhelpfully that she would make new ones. "Try it out for a year. It really is a great school and you'll be so close to Europe. Imagine where you could go sightseeing," she said, appealing to Khalilah's ambition to see the world.

"Just a year?" Khalilah looked at her dad for confirmation.

"If that's what you want," he answered.

"Okay," Khalilah sighed with obvious reluctance. "I suppose if it's *only* a year..."

But how would she tell her friends, and what would Maddie, Alana, and Sofia say?

CHAPTER 60

Change: The only constant

Maddie didn't do tears.

Not when the BlueJay Bruisers almost broke her leg in last year's game. Not when her first violin got stolen. Not even when the kids from the other school whispered insults or called her names as she walked past. Tears dry up fast when you take a blowtorch to your eyes. To burn images from your brain. Images like her dad lying in waste from cancer. Yellow. Dying.

If there had been a blowtorch.

Maddie was the strong one when she'd first met Alana on the *Kidz2Air* program at the community radio station. It was just after Alana's dad had died. She was the one to take the new girl under her wing and coax the smile back onto her face through shared playlists and exaggerated DJ accents. That both their dads were gone was the first thread to hold them together. It was a bond that had grown stronger and tighter ever since.

And now Maddie was off to The Con. Khalilah was moving to London. Sofia was doing a Summer Science Internship at the University of Melbourne. All but Alana were embarking on a new adventure. So why did Maddie feel like she was the one being abandoned?

Again.

Whatever.

Maddie didn't do tears.

...

"London's not that far, you know," Khalilah said. "It's like, you get on a plane, they feed you a couple of meals, you watch about five movies, and then you're there."

To Maddie who had never been farther than North Sydney, who didn't even own a passport, London was practically Mars.

Sofia looked at Khalilah in the mirror, through

the corner of one eye, because to look at her friend straight-on felt way too weird. "You look really different in your new head thingy." Khalilah's face was framed like an apple. It made her cheeks look rounder and her eyes look huge. Sofia remained wary about the change. As far as she was concerned, Khalilah's Auntie Nor was still the scariest nun she had ever met.

Khalilah scratched her head through the fabric. It felt itchy and uncomfortable. When she'd complained and said, "It's hot," Auntie Nor had said, "Hell is hot," and effectively shut down the conversation.

"We call it a *tudong*. It's pretty handy, too," Khalilah said with her characteristic grin. "See?" She held out the ear buds of her MP3 which were hiding under the silk scarf. If school got boring she was going to listen to Jet Tierbert. Maybe even if school *didn't* get boring.

"Plus, I figure 'Auntie Snore' doesn't really need to see my hair right now," Khalilah said, removing her headscarf to adjust it properly.

Khalilah's hair was such a violent orange it punched your eyes.

It was shaved on one side.

It was so neon it *glowed.*

"I mean, I know flight staff can deliver babies on planes, and all that," she continued to prattle as they all stared, "but they probably don't want to deal with a coronary. What?" she said when no one said a word. "I'm going to Lon-don, ba-by!" she said with Austin Power-swagger. "I'm blending in!"

For the first time that day, Maddie and Sofia smiled. They helped Khalilah put her tudong back on and adjusted the corners so they were even. Khalilah was still there. Under the tudong. Under the mad, neon hair. Even thousands of kilometers away in "Lon-don, ba-by," Khalilah wasn't going to change.

"You have a serious death wish," Sofia told her friend who just beamed in reply.

"Are you crying, Maddie?" Alana asked, amazed.

"Maddie doesn't do tears," Khalilah said emphatically.

Then there were no longer four heads, but one: a chocolate, magenta, electric blue, flaming patch of giggles and gasps and not-tears.

The End

Alana Oakley

BIOGRAPHY

Poppy Inkwell writes a lot of different things.

Stories...

Website content...

Mandalas...

But not Christmas cards ... or not very often.

When she's not at her desk writing, you will find her ferreting in car boot sales, experimenting with food gastronomy, or playing with her camera.

Born in the Philippines, she now lives by the beach in Australia with one husband, two of her children, and four pets (May They Rest In Peace).

See www.poppyinkwell.com for happenings, weird trivia, and more!

OTHER TITLES BY POPPY INKWELL IN THIS FABULOUS FUNNY MYSTERY SERIES:

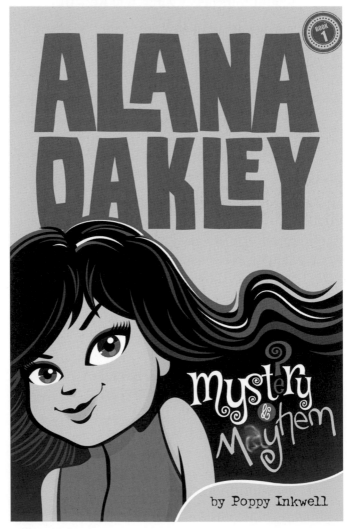

READY FOR ANYTHING?

The mysterious disappearance of a friend's precious charm sets the sassy sleuth, Alana Oakley, on the warpath. But Alana quickly realizes that having Attitude with a capital "A" isn't enough to solve the case – not when her first year at Gibson High has her dueling with the military-inspired Coach Kusmuk, dodging the over-exuberant Nurse Cathy, or deciphering dubious algebraic equations. If that wasn't enough to deal with, her impulsive and accident-prone mother is one click away from Internet-dating a mass murderer! Or a magician! Or worse! The biggest mystery of all is whether Alana's birthday wish will come true: Will this year be different or will it go horribly wrong, as usual?

Better call the fire department ... just in case.

OTHER TITLES BY POPPY INKWELL IN THIS FABULOUS FUNNY MYSTERY SERIES:

ALL FIRED UP?

Mysterious school fires get Alana Oakley hot under the collar, and she suspects the secretive new boy, Flynn, has something to do with them. But how can she prove it with her best friends drooling and fighting over the new Bad Boy? Then there's the problem of her mom's new boyfriend, Dr. Gray. Why does an "expert" on teen behavior have a creepy obsession with *dentistry*?! Is newbie Flynn the serial arsonist? Is Dr. Gray a modern Dr. Jekyll and Mr. Hyde? And will her birthday be another Epic Fail?

All will be revealed in the chaotic adventure Alana calls Life.